Readers love *Override*
by SJD PETERSON

"I loved this story. Little angst, no anger issues, no overblown drama, just two men finding a way to meet in the middle and merge their worlds."
　　—Alpha Book Club

"The strength of *Override* is definitely the strong and steady connection between Seth and Donavan and their growing romance."
　　　　—Sinfully Gay
　　　　Romance Book
　　　　Reviews

"…I like my stories with a good build-up, well portrayed characters, good chemistry, and bare minimum angst. This is exactly what I got here and I read it in one sitting, enjoying every page."
　　　　—Three Books Over the Rainbow

By SJD PETERSON

BAMF
Beyond Duty
Innocence to the Max
Leon
Masters & Boyd
My Hometown
A Night Never Forgotten
Plan B
Rival Within
With S.A. McAuley: Ruin Porn
Splintered
Tuck & Cover

GUARDS OF FOLSOM
Riveted
Pup
Tag Team
Pony
Roped
Mauled
Bound

WHISPERING PINES RANCH
Lorcan's Desire
Quinn's Need
Ty's Obsession
Conner's Courage
Jess's Journey

UNDERGROUND CLUB
Override
Limitless

Published by DREAMSPINNER PRESS
www.dreamspinnerpress.com

LIMITLESS

SJD PETERSON

Published by

DREAMSPINNER PRESS

5032 Capital Circle SW, Suite 2, PMB# 279, Tallahassee, FL 32305-7886 USA
www.dreamspinnerpress.com

Limitless
© 2016 SJD Peterson.

Cover Art
© 2016 Ronaldo Gutierrez, Photographer.
Cover Design
© 2016 Paul Richmond.
http://www.paulrichmondstudio.com
Cover content is for illustrative purposes only and any person depicted on the cover is a model.

ISBN: 978-1-63477-533-5
Digital ISBN: 978-1-63477-534-2
Library of Congress Control Number: 2016907026
Published December 2016
v. 1.0

Printed in the United States of America

This paper meets the requirements of
ANSI/NISO Z39.48-1992 (Permanence of Paper).

For my friend and editor Jason Bradley. Because of you,
this story had to be told.

Chapter One

NASH MEAD stood outside a nondescript door, his heart thumping rapidly and his skin tingling with anticipation. He closed his eyes and took several deep breaths, searching for a little calm. He was a Dom with a reputation for being stern; this place—the Underground Club—was his playground, and yet, he could control himself no better than a young, inexperienced pup. He hadn't been this worked up or this excited in…. *Fuck!* It had been years. He took in one more deep breath and held it before blowing it out slowly. He sought that peaceful place within him. Typically, he could call it up with ease, but tonight he was having a great deal of difficulty. He rolled his neck and squared his shoulders, then opened the door.

The scent of leather, sweat, and male arousal hung in the air. The distant thud of a flogger, the cries of pleasure-filled pain, moans, grunts and thumping bass filled the club, and the half-dressed men in tight leather completed the smorgasbord of sensual delights. Although Nash had been indulging in the rich offering of lust the Underground Club had to offer for years, recently his needs and desires had changed. It was as if he were entering the club for the first time, full of nervous energy and eagerness.

Standing near the entrance, Nash scanned the dimly lit room, seeking out the handsome face with lean, angular features and those bright green eyes that haunted his dreams.

A twinge of disappointment settled in his gut when he couldn't find the man he sought within the crowd. Troy always brought his boy to the club on Thursday nights. Perhaps it was too early. Nash checked his watch—*nine thirty*—they should have been here by now. Nash made his way to the bar, nodding to those who greeted him. He found a spot at the end and stood with his arms crossed over his chest and a scowl on his face. If that wasn't enough to keep others from approaching him, he was sure his dark, brooding attitude would do it.

He wasn't in the mood for pleasantries. He was a fucking mess. Hell, he'd been a mess for months, all due to Joshua.

Nash wasn't a rookie; he'd been a member of this club and living the lifestyle for close to a decade. He lived by a strict set of rules and demanded his submissives follow them to the letter. And yet, each time he laid eyes on Joshua, Nash wanted to run to him. He wanted to brush his fingers across the dark stubble on his jaw, taste those full lips and—codes of conduct be damned—steal him away from his Dom. There was little doubt that if he approached Troy and asked for permission to touch, to fuck and beat, the Dom would grant it. Troy often shared his submissives with others. However, Nash didn't dare ask. He wanted so much more than a scene, a single experience. He wanted to possess Joshua and make him his own.

He didn't understand this new obsession. It went far beyond the disrespect Nash had for Troy as a Dominant or the way he treated his boys—on the verge of abuse in Nash's opinion—although he was sure that was part of it. But from the first moment he'd seen Joshua's stunning green eyes, Nash had been a goner for the submissive. That night, Troy had embarrassed his boy, treated him as nothing more than a plaything to be quickly tossed aside rather than the precious gift Joshua was. It had taken every bit of control Nash could muster to keep from striking Troy and rescuing the boy.

A glimpse of a head covered in long black hair caused Nash's pulse to kick up. Even with the two-inch soles on his heavy black boots, his five-foot-ten-inch height put him at a disadvantage. He went up on tiptoes and craned his neck to see over the crowd. A smile curled his lip when he finally spotted the man he'd been seeking. Joshua wore loose-fitting jeans with a silver-studded black belt holding the pants up on his lean hips. Strips of broad black leather stretched across his well-defined chest and around to his back in the form of a V. The harness was held together by a two silver O-rings. One over his breast bone, the second one between his shoulder blades. Joshua was skinnier than Nash, but they were the same height.

"Good evening, Master Nash. Is there anything I can get for you?"

Nash cut a quick glance at the boy who had just appeared in front of him. Denny was a little wisp of a man, yet much stronger than he appeared and quite handsome. Nash had enjoyed the sub's company several times, but since fixating on Joshua, Nash simply hadn't been moved to take another.

"Thank you, boy, but I don't require anything tonight," Nash informed him without taking his gaze from Joshua. "If you'll excuse me."

Nash worked his way through the crowd, finding a spot on the far side of the club where he could lean against the wall and have the perfect vantage point from which to watch Joshua. The submissive kept his head down, his long hair obscuring his face, as he went to his knees gracefully next to the chair Troy had taken. A second, smaller man with longish blond hair who Nash didn't recognize knelt on the other side of Troy. To anyone else watching the trio, nothing would seem amiss. Troy often entered the club with two submissives. However, Nash had spent hours studying every nuance of Joshua's movements and demeanor and could tell something wasn't right.

Joshua's posture was always perfect, yet relaxed. Tonight there was palpable tension in his muscles and his hands were clasped so tightly behind his back, his knuckles were white. Nash had the uncanny feeling Joshua was hanging his head in shame rather than bowing it in respect.

Several minutes passed. Joshua didn't move, yet Nash's unease ratcheted up with each tick of the clock. Troy continually ran his fingers through the unknown sub's hair, occasionally bending down as if to speak to him, while completely ignoring Joshua. It took ironclad willpower on Nash's part not to stomp over and rescue Joshua from the isolation imposed upon him. But it wasn't Nash's place. Troy wasn't breaking any rules, and as much as Nash wished otherwise, Joshua wasn't his. Plus, Joshua was allowing his Dom to treat him in such a poor manner. Why didn't he safeword or simply get up and walk away? It was beyond Nash's comprehension, but obviously the mistreatment must have been acceptable to Joshua since he allowed it week after week.

Suddenly and without provocation, Troy palmed Joshua's head and pulled it back. The angry expression on Troy's face and the fear on Joshua's had Nash pushing off the wall before he thought better of it and heading to the table.

Upon reaching the trio, Nash overheard Troy spit, "Why the fuck can't you make me look as good as Mark does?"

Although rage was coursing through him, Nash kept his features neutral and slid casually into the chair opposite Troy. "Evening, Troy. Mind if I join you?"

Troy snapped his head up, his angry expression morphing into one of surprise, but he recovered quickly and smiled. He released his hold on Joshua's head and patted it as he said, "Considering you've already taken a seat, be my guest."

"Sorry for being so bold, but I couldn't help but notice your boy and wanted to compliment you on such masculine perfection. You must be very proud of him."

Troy's smile grew, his cocky attitude firmly in place when he laid his hand on his other boy's shoulder. "Why yes I am. He is quite lovely, isn't he?"

"Oh, he's beautiful," Nash agreed. He nodded toward Joshua. "But I meant him."

"What?"

The look on Troy's face was priceless. For the second time, Nash had surprised the arrogant bastard, and he couldn't help but grin. "He caught my eye the moment you entered the club. His posture is exemplary and the way he so gracefully went to his knees…." Nash cocked his head and stared at Joshua as if he were considering his words, but it was all for dramatic effect. He already knew what he was going to say. He looked up and met Troy's stunned gaze. "You wouldn't by chance be willing to share him with me tonight, would you? I have an itch I do believe he may be able to scratch."

Troy's brow furrowed, a disbelieving expression on his face as he looked back and forth between Nash and Joshua. How could the bastard not see how handsome Joshua was?

Troy's gaze settled on Nash, and his arrogant demeanor returned. He leaned back in his chair and waved his hand dismissively at Joshua. "Take him. Do what you want. I have no use for him tonight."

The anger flared again, and Nash put his hands beneath the table and clenched them into fists to control the urge to slap the asshole upside his idiot skull. Wasn't Troy going to set rules or boundaries? It didn't matter that Nash had an excellent reputation within the club. It was Troy's responsibility always to think of his submissive's safety first. There was so much he wanted to say and do, but instead he went to his feet and gritted out, "Thank you, I appreciate your generosity."

"You're welcome." Troy turned to Joshua. "Go with Master Nash and do as he tells you. If I get a less-than-favorable report, you will pay considerably for your disrespect. Is that understood?"

"Yes, Sir," Joshua responded quietly. He went to his feet, keeping his head low.

Nash made his way to the bar, Joshua silently walking to heel. On the way, Nash took the opportunity to calm himself. He was beyond pissed at Troy, but now that he had finally gotten the chance to spend time with Joshua, Nash refused to let his ire drive him.

"Good evening. What can I get for you, Master Nash?" Conrad, the bartender, asked.

"Evening, boy. Could you retrieve me a key as well as two bottles of water?"

"Yes, sir. The King's Suite is currently the only room we have available. But if you'd like to wait, I believe the Whipping Room will be available shortly."

"The suite is fine."

Nash thrummed his fingers against the polished wood surface as he discreetly studied Joshua in the mirror behind the bar. The irritation swirling through Nash was not Joshua's fault, and it would be unfair to take it out on him. He took the opportunity to let Joshua's nearness drain the ill temperament from him. By the time Conrad handed him the key and water bottles, he'd been able to rein in his anger and allow his excitement at getting Joshua to flow through him.

Once again, Joshua followed him. Nash didn't have to look behind him to see the boy; he could feel his presence close to his back. Nash unlocked the door and swung it open. "After you."

Hands clasped behind his back, Joshua did as he was told, going to the center of the room. He adjusted his stance, pushed out his chest, and waited for instructions.

Nash closed and locked the door, then set the key on the small table near the entryway. "Have a seat and relax."

"Sir?" Joshua sounded confused.

"Which didn't you understand? The have-a-seat part or the relaxing part?"

"Both, Sir," Joshua admitted. "Where would you like me to sit?"

Nash studied the room. There was a large four-poster king-size bed covered in luxurious dark burgundy silk and an ornate armoire Nash knew was stocked with supplies as well as numerous dildos and plugs. The room also contained a small sitting area comprised of two leather wingback chairs separated by a beautifully carved wooden table. The whole room from the furniture to the fine art on the walls was a bit over-the-top for Nash's taste. He'd been in the room only a few times when, like tonight, it was the only one available. He briefly considered having Joshua sit on the bed, then just as quickly dismissed the idea. Joshua plus the bed was too much of a temptation.

"You may take one of the chairs," Nash told him.

"Yes, Sir." Joshua did as instructed. It took him a moment to find the correct position, finally settling on entwining his fingers and resting his hands on his lap. He followed only part of Nash's order. Joshua was far from relaxed, but Nash supposed it couldn't be helped. He doubted anyone had ever given the submissive such a command.

Nash sat in the empty chair and set the water bottles on the table. "Does your master often share you without setting guidelines?"

Joshua visibly stiffened. Even though his head was bowed, his long hair hiding his features from Nash, the panic in the boy was palpable. "I… I'm sorry, Sir. I'm not sure how to answer that."

"Honestly. Before you answer, tuck your hair behind your ears. I wish to see your face."

"Yes, sir." Joshua did as he was instructed. Nash was now able to see the worry and confusion etched on Joshua's face. "I don't know what guidelines you speak of, Sir. I don't make the rules. I only follow them."

"Yes, but you would know if he has done this before. Has he given you to another Dom without asking that Dom what his intentions were or setting clear boundaries?"

Joshua swallowed, then pursed his lips. "I don't question him, Sir."

Nash blew out a heavy breath. "Are you comfortable with the arrangement?"

"Yes, Sir."

Nash knew Joshua was lying. The way he had hesitated before answering was telling. "So you do not care about your safety?"

"Master Troy knows what's right for me."

"Bullshit!" Nash jumped to his feet and began pacing. "Don't you realize he's putting you in danger? He didn't even bother to ask me what I planned on doing with you. You think that's caring about your fucking safety?"

"I... I...." Joshua began to tremble and seemed to shrink into himself. "Please don't ask me to speak poorly of Master Troy. I... I can't, Sir."

Nash stopped and stared at the devastated-looking Joshua. The man was wringing his hands and shaking. The anger instantly drained from Nash. *What the hell am I doing?* He was going about this all wrong. Questioning a submissive about his Dominant was crossing a line. He had no proof Troy was abusing Joshua, only a suspicion. He should be demanding these answers from Troy, not tormenting his submissive.

"I'm sorry, I shouldn't have asked you such things."

Joshua was well trained. He didn't respond since Nash hadn't asked him a direct question. No way had this been Troy's doing. He'd only been bringing the boy into the club for the past couple of months. Nash was damn sure going to find out who had trained Joshua and how he had come to belong to Troy. Nash's first instinct was to grab Joshua, wrap him in a hug, and ease the tension from his body. Instead, he returned to his chair and took a bottle of water, twisting off the cap and downing a good amount. He needed to figure out how to get the answers he wanted without distressing Joshua further. But how?

"Would you like some water?" Nash offered.

"No thank you, Sir."

Nash studied Joshua for a moment. He seemed to have settled a bit now that Nash was no longer grilling him with questions about his master. He was far from done, though. He planned to get to the bottom of what the hell Joshua was doing with an asshole like Troy, but he'd find out in another place and time, and then it wouldn't be

Joshua who would be withstanding Nash's interrogation. Instead, he set those need-to-know questions aside and asked Joshua some easier, more generic questions.

"How old are you?"

"Twenty-five, Sir."

"Are you h—" Nash started to ask him if he was happy but snapped his mouth shut. That was another unfair question. He ran his fingers through his hair and blew out a frustrated breath. *Fuck!* How much was this truly about Joshua rather than Nash's crazy obsession with the man?

"Your accent says you're from the south."

After a long silence, Nash realized he hadn't asked Joshua a question. Man, he was rattled. He needed to get his shit together. "Where are you from?"

"Tennessee, Sir."

Nash smiled. He liked the lilt of Joshua's voice when he wasn't so panicked. It was dark, whiskey smooth, and like a kiss against Nash's skin. "Beautiful country in Tennessee. Why on earth would you want to move to Flint, Michigan?"

"I came here with my Dom, Sir."

"And your Dom gave you to Master Troy?"

Joshua's shoulders slumped and the sadness radiating off him was unmistakable. "No, Sir. I…. If you don't… I mean…." He blew out a heavy breath. "Sorry, Sir."

Nash's gut twisted. He'd thought he was doing the right thing by rescuing Joshua from the way Troy was treating him in the club and here he was tormenting the poor man.

"Dammit, I'm sorry. I shouldn't have pried into your personal life." He patted his shirt pocket, searching for a smoke—a habit he'd given up nearly a year ago, but Christ would he love to have one at the moment. Joshua wasn't the only one who was nervous. Nash picked at the label on the water bottle instead while he contemplated what to say next. This was completely new territory for him. He'd never been affected so deeply by a stranger and had never been so out of sorts. It was both exciting and maddening in equal measures.

A long silence followed. Finally, Nash said, "I'm fucking this up, aren't I?"

"Sir?"

"I can't take all the credit for my irrational behavior tonight. Some of the blame falls on your shoulders, you know?"

"Sir?" Joshua repeated, his voice rising in apparent alarm.

"If you weren't so fucking stunning, I might be able to focus a bit more. It's hard to think when the blood my brain so obviously needs has pooled in my groin."

He'd never seen Joshua look as happy as he did upon hearing Nash's compliment. The curl of lip hit Nash directly in the center of his chest. He could only imagine what effect a full-on smile would have on him.

"I'm quite serious, you know?" Nash added. "You are by far one of the most handsome men I have ever had the pleasure of meeting."

"Thank you, Sir, but I'm just me."

"Hmm and modest too. I like that. So what kind of tale shall we come up with to relay to your master? I would hate for you to be punished on my account."

Joshua tilted his head. Nash could see he was trying to sneak a look at him, but his training didn't allow him to lift his face or look Nash directly in the eye. "Tale, Sir?"

"I brought you back here on a whim. I shouldn't have intervened between you and your master. I understand that now. But I have no use for your body tonight."

Once again Joshua's shoulders slumped, and the happy expression was instantly gone.

"Not that I wouldn't love to," Nash amended quickly. God, how he wanted to, but not like this. The Dom/sub relationship was based on mutual needs and pleasures. And yet, strange as it seemed, Nash felt as if he'd be using Joshua. "I brought you back here under false pretenses and for that, I do apologize."

"No apology needed, Sir. I only wish to please you, Sir."

Nash considered Joshua's offer for a moment. "There is one thing you can do for me. Stand and display in the center of the room."

Joshua stood and strolled to the center of the room. Nash gave him a moment to get into position before he pushed to his feet and moved close to Joshua, getting his first up close and personal look. Nash swallowed down a gasp when he found several white scars that covered Joshua's back, including numerous discolored keloids covering the lumbar area as well as both shoulders. Nash moved to stand in front of Joshua, the remnants of old wounds continuing across the man's chest and down both arms. Nash didn't know whether to rage or cry at the roadmap of abuse to such beautiful skin.

Nash ran the tip of his index finger over a recently healed mark below Joshua's navel. "Who did this to you?" His voice cracked with a swell of conflicting emotions.

"I made a mistake and was properly disciplined, Sir."

Jesus fuck, this roadmap of torture across Joshua's body wasn't proper anything. It was so beyond okay. Nash was having a difficult time processing what he was seeing. He also had no idea what to say. So instead, he said nothing, not trusting himself to say something that wouldn't upset Joshua further than he already had. He would be looking into this; it was far from over, but not now, not at this moment. "You will please me by giving me a kiss."

"A kiss, Sir?"

"You do know what a kiss is, don't you?"

"Yes, Sir, it's just…." Joshua shifted slightly, no doubt a nervous habit, but he caught himself quickly and straightened his spine and stilled. "No one has ever asked for me to kiss them."

"Do you have a problem with my request?"

"No, Sir. Not at all. I would very much like to please you with a kiss."

Nash had to bend his knees to press his lips to Joshua's since his head was bowed. The instant their mouths met, an electrical jolt shot down Nash's spine, nearly stopping his breath. With the tips of his fingers, he lifted Joshua's chin so he could deepen the kiss. Joshua's lips parted, and Nash dove in, tasting and exploring with relish. Nash thread his fingers through Joshua's silky hair, holding him close.

The urge to take it further, to lay Joshua down on the bed and take what he desired, what he needed, was overwhelming, and Nash ended the kiss before he gave in to it. He took a step back, getting a glimpse of Joshua's bright green eyes before he lowered them.

Once again, Nash was hit with the urge to strip Joshua, cover his body with his own, look into those beautiful eyes, and bring them both to a new level of pleasure. *You are a fool.* He spun on his heels and retrieved the water bottles, tossing them in the trash before moving to the door. He picked up his keys and unlocked the door.

"I'm sorry I made you feel uncomfortable. Come along, I'll take you back to your master."

Nash opened the door, aware of Joshua behind him. Nash struggled with keeping his feet moving. He hated the fact that he had to return Joshua to his asshole Dom. Hopefully, if everything worked to his advantage, this would be the last time.

"Done already?" Troy asked as Nash approached the table. "I take it you didn't find him as pleasing as you thought."

The disdain in Troy's voice caused Nash to want to commit murder, but he stubbornly pushed the urge down and kept his voice neutral and his expression even. "He brought me immense pleasure with his mouth." Nash waited until Joshua was once again kneeling at his master's side before Nash moved around to the other end of the table. He leaned down and whispered in Troy's ear. "If you put one more scar on his flesh, it will be you I will take my pleasure from."

Troy pushed to his feet, his chest puffed out and a sneer curling his lip. "Who the hell do you think you are to tell me what I can and cannot do with my boy?"

Troy had a few inches on Nash, as well as a good twenty pounds, but Nash wasn't intimidated nor would he back down. He curled his hand into a fist, his nails digging into his palm with the effort it took not to throw a punch. He couldn't be this close to Troy and not succumb to violence. "Abuse him and see what happens."

With that, Nash walked away. Everything in him screamed for him to take Joshua with him, but he couldn't. He would soon, but he couldn't go into this blindly. He needed to find out what he could about Joshua. Knowledge was power, and Nash was all about power.

Chapter Two

DAMN, HE needed a drink. *A stiff one. Better yet, two stiff ones.* Nash ran his fingers through his damp brown hair, the longer strands of his fauxhawk sticking to his forehead. He did his best to put himself together, but whether he succeeded, he didn't have a clue. Inside he was a mess; he could only hope his inner turmoil didn't show in his features. He headed to the bar, surprised to see his old friend and the owner of the Underground, Malcolm Hodges. At forty-one, Malcolm was nearly ten years Nash's senior but one wouldn't know it to look at him. Malcolm's thick salt-and-pepper hair was cut in a modern pompadour, and other than a few laugh lines around his blue eyes, his olive skin was smooth and flawless. He also kept up with the latest fashion trends, but when Malcolm was at the club, he wore his signature tailored black suit, ever the stylish-looking gentleman. Nash slid onto the stool next to him. "I didn't expect to see you tonight," he said by way of greeting as he patted Malcolm on the back. "You look well."

"Yes, well, looks can be deceiving. Ten days with my family has made me completely crazy."

"You come by it naturally," Nash teased. "How are they doing?"

Malcolm sighed dramatically. "Mother refused to go to rehab because she'd miss senior citizen's day at the casino. I told her if she could get up and walk to the car, I'd allow her to go."

"And?"

Malcolm gave Nash an aggrieved look. "Crazy woman had a double knee replacement and tried to leave the hospital. Luckily Aunt Ester had hidden Mom's clothes. Ester, by the way, informed me she has been praying each Sunday for my damned soul."

"That was big of her."

"I thought so," Malcolm replied with a shrug. "What are you drinking?"

"Whiskey."

Malcolm arched a brow at him. "That bad?"

"You have no idea."

"I can't wait to hear this." Malcolm waved a hand at Conrad. "Boy, bring me a bottle of whiskey and two glasses."

"Two?" Nash inquired.

"Yes, I figure if you need it, then I'm going to need it by the time you tell me your reasoning. Save the poor boy a trip."

"I'm not even sure of my fucking reasoning," Nash grumbled.

"Considering the angry vibes coming from you after you spent time with Troy's boy, I'd say it was something important."

"The man just rubs me the wrong way is all," Nash hedged.

"Hold that thought."

Conrad set two glasses and a bottle of Irish whiskey in front of them. "Would you like me to pour them for you, Sir?"

"No, thank you. Run along, boy, private conversation here."

"Yes, Sir."

Malcolm filled each glass with a good measure and threw his drink back before refilling it. He slid the other glass toward Nash. "Now you may continue."

Nash swirled the light amber liquid in his glass before taking a sip. The fruity flavor transitioned to something more earthy and salty. It was very smooth and warmed Nash all the way to his gut. "This is wonderful." Nash took another sip.

"Yes, yes, I'll have a bottle sent to you. Now back to the conversation at hand. You know how I despise not being in the know."

Nash set his glass down and looked over at Malcolm pointedly. "What do you know about Troy's new submissive, Joshua?"

"Not a lot."

Nash regarded Malcolm for a moment and then downed the rest of his drink. "I think Troy may be abusing him."

Malcolm appeared to be stunned. "Did Joshua tell you that?"

Nash poured himself another healthy shot and took it with him when he sat back in his chair. "No, he didn't say anything against his Dom. Call it a gut instinct."

"You know I trust you and your gut, but I have to ask, are you sure your opinion isn't…." Malcolm waved his hand around. "You know, due to your dislike of Troy?"

Nash swirled his whiskey, staring at the movement of the liquid as he considered Malcolm's question. It was true he had never been a fan of Troy's. Upon meeting the man, Nash had walked away with a lingering distaste. Troy was arrogant, rude, and a complete asshole, often looking down his nose at others. This was no doubt partly due to his upbringing, being a trust-fund baby. The fucker didn't know what it meant to put in an honest day's work. Nash also didn't approve of the way Troy treated his submissives, but who was he to judge what two consenting adults did together? Humiliation wasn't something he was into, neither personally nor as something he would ever subject a submissive to. His distaste for the practice didn't make it wrong. Be that as it may, he was envious of Troy. Nash could easily admit that he was smitten with Joshua. He supposed it was possible that he was allowing his emotions to cloud his judgment. But the scars on Joshua's flesh spoke otherwise. Nash couldn't ignore the nagging feeling that Joshua was, in fact, being abused.

"I don't know, I guess that could be part of it," Nash finally admitted.

"And yet, your suspicion lingers."

Nash nodded. "I have no proof, but I intend to look into the matter further."

"What can I do to help?"

Nash looked up and met Malcolm's gaze. "You honor me, old friend."

"I've known you for many years, and you aren't one to make frivolous accusations. If you say something is going on, I believe you. Besides, you know I won't stand for anyone being abused within this club, nor could I idly sit by and allow it outside of these walls if I can help it."

"You're a good man, Malcolm. I hope I'm wrong about this, but I don't think so." Nash took a sip of his whiskey. "If you could see what you can find out about Joshua, I'd much appreciate it. I know he came to Michigan from Tennessee with his old Dom. I need to know who that was and how he ended up with Troy. Also, who he's played with, his likes, dislikes."

"I'll see what I can discover."

"Oh, stop being so coy." Nash patted Malcolm's arm and chuckled. "You're like a bloodhound when you want information. I have no doubt you'll find it all out. You'll probably be able to tell me what size his dick is."

"Six and a half inches."

It was Nash's turn to be stunned. "And you know this how? You said you barely knew anything about the man."

Malcolm waved his hand flippantly. "The boy wears very tight pants from time to time. I have eyes. I also regard myself as a cock connoisseur."

"A cock connoisseur? Are you serious?" Nash laughed.

"Quite serious," Malcolm remarked with a sly grin.

Nash shook his head, then raised his glass. Malcolm clinked his against it, his smile growing. Nash took another drink, slower this time. It would do him no good to get sloshed. He wasn't a very pleasant drunk, and with the irritation churning in his gut, the whiskey would be fuel for a very unpleasant eruption.

"Oh, I just remembered," Malcolm said suddenly. "I've heard rumors that Joshua hooked up with Kirk when he first arrived in Flint. Now, I don't know if they are true. You know how this lot loves to gossip. But it wouldn't hurt to ask him. He's at the other end of the bar." He nodded in that direction.

"Kirk?" Nash asked, astonished. Kirk Gaines was one of the kinkiest sons of bitches Nash had ever met. His likes bordered on truly perverse. He was also into dishing out some hardcore pain. The bullwhip was one of Kirk's favorite implements. "What in the hell would Joshua be doing with the likes of him?"

"The love of pain?" Malcolm suggested. "But as I said, it's merely a rumor."

Nash drained his glass and stood up. "Only one way to find out if it's true." He adjusted his clothes, poured himself another drink, and headed to the end of the bar.

"Good evening, Kirk." Nash took the seat next to him.

"Hey, Nash. How are you doing tonight? Finding any action that suits you?"

"Not looking for action, only answers."

Kirk eyed Nash's drink and then met his gaze. "I never trust the answers I find in booze."

"Nor do I. Rumor has it you've played with Joshua before?"

"Troy's new boy?" Kirk asked.

Nash nodded and sipped his drink.

"Yeah, I played with him once and that was enough for me." Kirk looked unnerved as he ran his fingers through his long grayish beard, suddenly looking every bit of his forty-five years. "Trust me, that's a hornet's nest you do *not* want to get tangled up in. That boy is a complete and utter fucking mess."

Damn, Nash hadn't expected that type of reaction to the mention of Joshua's name. Still, he wasn't deterred, his interest in the submissive all the more piqued. "What do you mean by mess?"

"He has no limits. Like zero fucking limits."

"That's impossible. Everyone has their limits."

"Not Joshua. He's as bad as a heroin junkie, only his drug of choice is pain. He's constantly looking for the bigger and better high. He'll let you kill him before he'll safeword."

Nash propped his elbow on the bar and ran his goatee through his thumb and index finger as he considered Kirk's words. If Joshua were a pain junkie, it could be a whole lot worse than a nest of swarming bugs. A submissive who required that much work wasn't what Nash was looking to get into. He hadn't had a full-time sub for many years and wasn't sure he wanted one. To push a submissive to his limits was one thing, but to try and teach them limits when they had none was a whole other kind of hardship. Did he want to take on such a responsibility? He cut a glance toward Joshua, who was still kneeling at Troy's feet and still being ignored. *Fuck!* The way his chest tightened when he looked at the man, Nash already knew the answer. He would do everything in his power to see that Joshua wasn't abused and that he didn't suffer one more mark of a Dom gone too far.

Nash picked up his glass and raised it as he stood. "Thank you for the information. I appreciate it."

"No problem. Seriously, Nash, think about what I said long and hard before you consider playing with that boy. He may not have limits, but I assure you, he will push you to yours."

"I've taken it to heart." Nash nodded. "Have a pleasant evening."

"Same to you."

It was worse than Nash had thought. A pain slut addicted to the high with no limits? *Jesus!* Even as he thought it, Nash knew it was true. He'd seen the look in Kirk's eyes—pure fear. If Joshua scared someone like Kirk, it was only a matter of time before Joshua ended up on a stainless steel slab. It wasn't unheard of that such a submissive in the hands of the wrong Dom could lose their life in their quest for the bigger high. Joshua was a ticking time bomb.

Nash's stomach was in knots. His head swam as he walked back across the bar toward Malcolm. A pain junkie? *Jesus.* The term was loosely and often times incorrectly used. There was a huge difference between someone who enjoyed pleasure-filled pain and someone addicted to it. The body was an amazing thing. During times of trauma, the brain released endorphins. In controlled situations, the use of pain for pleasure could produce a chemical high similar to morphine. It was that high that pushed someone who enjoyed pain to one who not only craved it but needed it until it became a full-on addiction. Or he could be suffering from an algolagnic disorder rather than being a true pain junkie. Yeah, there was a lot to think about before rushing in and snatching up Joshua, so many fucking variables that it made his head hurt.

Distracted, Nash didn't even notice his good friend and fellow Dom Seth until he stood in front of him. Seth said, "You look like hell, are you okay?"

"Yes, I'm fine. No, honestly, I'm not, but it's good to see you." He pulled Seth into a hug and patted his back. "I don't mean to interrupt."

"Nonsense," Seth assured him. "Have a seat." He encouraged Nash to take his stool and moved down to the next one.

Nash turned to Malcolm. "I'm disappointed in you, old man."

Malcolm put his hand over his heart, looking as if Nash had wounded him. "What? What have I done to make you feel this way?"

"You have a submissive within your club who may end up being taken out in a body bag," Nash informed him, his tone sad even to his own ears.

"Now it is I who doesn't want to interrupt. Would you like me to give you a moment alone with Malcolm?" Seth offered.

"No, no, stay," Nash responded. "I'd like to hear your thoughts and I respect your opinion." He and Seth had been friends for years, although not as long as he and Malcolm had, as Malcolm had been the one to introduce them. But Seth was a good man, a respectable one, and a friend he trusted.

Seth patted his shoulder. "I'd be more than happy to help if I can."

"Are you saying Joshua is in danger?" Malcolm squeaked in surprise.

Nash nodded. "He's a pain junkie, his body covered with scars, and he scared the living hell out of Kirk after only one scene."

"Dear Lord," Malcolm muttered. "I… I'm not even sure what to say. You know I do a thorough background check on every Dom, but I never thought to do the same on the boys they bring in."

"I'm sure you did," Seth assured Malcolm. "But who is this Joshua and to whom does he belong?"

"Seth is right. This isn't your fault, Malcolm." Nash took Malcolm's drink and downed it. "Joshua is a new sub who I believe Troy is abusing. I was talking to Kirk about him, and after discovering the extent of Joshua's issues, I'm pissed that Kirk didn't inform you. He had an obligation to do so and failed. I'm also beyond pissed that Joshua is with the likes of Troy."

"I agree with Kirk's failure, but Troy is a highly skilled, very popular Dom," Malcolm pointed out.

"I—"

Malcolm interrupted Nash by holding up his hand. "I know you don't always agree with his practices, but he's never crossed a line, and I've gotten nothing but favorable feedback from the boys he's played with in the past."

"Malcolm is right," Seth added. "I've known Troy for a couple of years and you're right, his practices aren't always, shall we say, appropriate, but don't let your personal dislike of him and those practices cause you to rush to judgment so quickly. Perhaps Joshua is content with him?"

"Content isn't the same as happy."

"And you think you can make this boy happy?" Malcolm answered his own question. "You're not sure you can."

"I didn't say that," Nash replied.

"You didn't have to. You have a tell."

"A tell?"

Malcolm pointed at Nash's goatee. "You pull on it whenever you're unsure. Don't ever play poker, or at least shave that thing off beforehand."

Nash folded his arms and laid them on the bar. "Yeah, I'm not real confident I could. Hell, I'm not even sure I want to take on anything that intense."

"It would be a full-time job." Malcolm thrummed his fingers on the bar. "Then there is the fact that Joshua has a Dom. That being said, it makes sense why Troy is displaying anger when interacting with Joshua. Troy has an ego, and if he didn't break him, I could see how that would send him into a tizzy."

"You think if you explain the situation to Troy, he will allow you to take Joshua on?" Seth suggested.

Before Nash could respond, Malcolm answered for him. "I have a feeling Troy would allow it, but Nash has pointed out that he isn't sure he wants to take the boy on."

"I don't, I mean, I did, but…." Nash pinched the bridge of his nose and huffed out a breath. "I don't even know what the fuck I'm feeling at the moment."

"Why don't you go home, give it some thought, and let me talk to Troy and find out what I can about Joshua? Feel him out, so to speak," Malcolm offered.

"Yeah, that's probably a good idea." He shoved his empty glass away. "This isn't a decision I should be making while under the influence of alcohol."

"Wise choice." Seth patted Nash on the back. "Give it a couple of days. That should give you enough time to do some soul-searching."

Nash nodded. "Thank you both," he said, looking to Malcolm and Seth. "I truly appreciate having a couple of level heads in this matter, as well as the sound advice."

"I'll have Mel take you home," Malcolm offered.

"Thank you." Nash stood and pulled his wallet from his back pocket.

Malcolm waved him off. "My treat. Now go home, get some rest, and we will talk soon."

Seth pulled him into a hug. "It was good seeing you again. I'm sure you'll do the right thing in this matter. I have the utmost faith and trust in you."

Nash was a little unsteady on his feet when Seth released him.

"C'mon, I'll walk you out." Malcolm patted Nash on the back. He turned to Seth. "I'll be right back. If you'd like to head to the dining room, I will join you there."

"Take your time," Seth responded.

Reluctantly, Nash turned his gaze away from Joshua and allowed Malcolm to lead him out of the club. He was a bit dazed from the turn of events, the alcohol, and the weight of the challenges he was about to take on. Even with his hesitation and reservations, he still wanted Joshua, more so now with the new information, if that were possible. Damn, he was a crazy fucker.

After saying good night to his friend, Nash sat in the back of Malcolm's car, staring out at the city but not seeing anything except Joshua's face. Those bright green eyes were calling to him. Nash's mind raced, stomach churning and heart hurting. He couldn't have known what he was getting into that first moment he'd spotted Joshua. Now that he did? Hornet's nest was an understatement, but even if he was worried about what was to come, he knew he was going to do anything within his power to help Joshua.

Chapter Three

BRUSH IN hand, Nash stared at the canvas as he had off and on for the last hour without adding a single stroke. The portrait was unfinished, but the eyes were complete—sorrow-filled eyes. He sat back on his stool and set the brush aside, giving up on the painting. Even though he could recall every line easily, the subject's face vivid in his mind, he found it fitting that the painting he'd started over a month ago remain unfinished.

"A work in progress." He supposed the statement could describe himself as well as Joshua.

Since returning from the club two nights ago, he'd thought of little else. The only problem was that he hadn't come up with any solutions to the clusterfuck he now found himself in. He had no idea how to bring a real pain junkie back from the edge. He discovered limits, pushed them, but he didn't set them. How the hell did you teach someone who had no boundaries?

With a frustrated grunt, he pushed up off his stool and turned away from the portrait. All this obsessing, planning, and thinking could be for nothing. Troy might not give up his boy. They might have a contract. Hell, it was quite possible, Joshua was happy with his Dom. Nash seriously doubted it, but what the hell did he know? Nash had no clue. He barely knew Joshua. He was going on gut instinct, but that wasn't the same as fact. He'd been wrong before.

"Maybe, maybe, and more fucking maybes," he grumbled.

There were too many variables to begin even working out a plan. Nash was all about lists, outlines, spreadsheets, and a clear and precise plan. He could do none of those until he heard from Malcolm. Nash stomped over to his workbench and snatched up his cell to check the display. Of course it was blank, just as it was when he'd checked it ten minutes ago.

He started to slam it back down but then jumped when it chirped. He checked the display again and sighed in relief when he saw Malcolm's name displayed. He pushed the On button.

"It's about time you called. I've been going out of my damn mind."

"Good evening to you too. I'm well, thank you for asking," Malcolm drawled.

"Sorry, I'm a little on edge."

"Understandable. Would you like to talk about what I've learned over the phone or would you rather I send a car for you? I have a lovely new bottle of scotch we could discuss it over."

The tension Nash had been experiencing for the last two days tightened further and his head began to throb. He rubbed the back of his neck, trying to alleviate the pain. "Are you saying I'm going to need a drink?"

"I think we both could use one. Mel will be there within the half hour."

Nash started to ask Malcolm to give him a hint of what he'd learned but decided against it. Getting only a partial story would probably be worse on his already-frayed nerves. "I'll see you soon."

Nash ended the call and ran his hand over his stubbled chin, the goatee—the tell—gone. He knew Malcolm would still be able to sense what he was feeling; they'd been close for years. However, when—or rather, if—he took on Joshua, Nash needed to be able to keep his emotions from showing. A submissive like Joshua could use those telltale signs of uncertainty against his Dom to get what he wanted.

"Goddammit, there you go again, planning without any details."

Frustrated, Nash did his best to let it go, pushed it down long enough to get to the club without totally freaking out. He took a quick shower, dressed in jeans, T-shirt, and casual boots and was ready to go when Mel showed up.

The ride into the city took about twenty minutes, and Nash used the time to reflect on what was going on and how he'd arrived at this moment.

Nash had always prided himself on his ability to stay levelheaded even in the most stressful of situations and never been what people would call obsessive. Sure he was a little anal, meticulous about the cleanliness of his home and personal hygiene. He was also a control freak, a trait he'd learned from his father. But he'd never been one to allow his emotions to rule over his good sense. That changed the moment he'd seen Joshua. Nash had no idea what it was about the submissive that had him turned into knots. It went well beyond attraction or reason.

Sweat beaded on Nash's forehead, and he rolled down the window, allowing the fresh breeze to swirl around the town car. He leaned his head back and closed his eyes. He tried to find some solace in the fact that he was about to get at least some answers to his questions, good or bad. It did little to quiet his nerves, however, or alleviate his unease that had settled in days ago. By the time he made it into the club, he was filled with both trepidation and excitement, the dual sensations causing him to tremble. He clamped down on his muscles and concentrated on keeping his steps measured and sure. Ignoring the other club members, Nash headed directly to Malcolm's office. He found Malcolm reclining in his chair, drink in hand. A bottle of scotch and a full glass sat on the coffee table.

"I see you've already poured me a drink," Nash said. "Am I to assume this means I'm not going to like what you have to say?"

Malcolm stood and handed one of the drinks to Nash. "This is thirty-five-dollar-an-ounce scotch. It's appropriate for good or bad news." He clinked his glass against Nash's. "Cheers."

Nash threw back his drink, the alcohol smooth and warming as it went down. "That is quite delicious." He flopped down onto the black leather sofa, rolling his empty glass in his fingers. "What have you found out about Joshua?"

"Right to the matter of business, huh?" Malcolm returned to his chair opposite of the couch.

"I've been going nuts so you'll have to forgive me if I bypass the pleasantries. Besides, I can tell by the look on your face you're about to burst with the knowledge you've obtained."

"Well, you know I do love a good story full of mystery, angst, and intrigue."

Nash reached for his nonexistent goatee but then quickly dropped his hand to his side. "I'm not sure I like the sound of this."

Malcolm arched a brow, obviously catching Nash with his tell. Malcolm grinned knowingly, picked up the carafe, and poured them both another drink. "Some you will like, but other things, I regret, not so much."

Nash swirled the scotch in his glass. "Hit me with the stuff I will like first, if you please."

"You were right about Troy."

"Everyone knows Troy is an asshole," Nash sniffed.

"Now, now. I know you don't always agree with his tactics. Your personalities simply do not mesh. Troy may be harsh at times, a little arrogant, but he is also a reasonable man."

"And how is he being reasonable in this situation?" Nash asked, doing his best to keep his dislike of Troy from coming out in the tone of his voice.

He apparently failed because Malcolm shook his head. "Troy has quite the ego as you are well aware."

"That's an understatement," Nash mumbled behind his glass, then took a sip. "How was I right about Troy?"

"That he wasn't the right Dom for Joshua. Troy admitted that he had no idea as to the depths of Joshua's problems. He was under the assumption that Joshua was simply a very naughty boy who purposefully pushed him. When Troy was unable to break him, his reaction to his failure was irritation and perhaps even anger."

"I—"

"Stop. I know what you are going to say, and I can assure you, he did not cause a single one of those scars you discovered. Yes, Troy should have done his research. He was a fool to take someone like Joshua on without a full understanding of the complexity of the sub's issues, and I have reprimanded him for this. However, he has agreed to terminate the six-month contract he has with Joshua if—"

Excitement surged through Nash, and he forgot his manners. "First thing Troy has done that I agree with. I have to say, he's not the total idiot I thought he was."

"Nash," Malcolm said sternly. "If you will stop interrupting me and allow me to finish you may not be so exuberant about the situation."

Uh-oh. He didn't like the tone of Malcolm's voice nor the aggrieved look in his eyes. "Sorry, please continue."

"Troy will relinquish his rights to Joshua and the boy has agreed with one stipulation."

"Which is? Wait a minute, don't answer that yet." Nash downed his scotch and poured another. "Now you may continue."

"I am rubbing off on you," Malcolm chuckled.

"We haven't done that in years," Nash reminded him.

"Ah yes, the good ol' days when you were but a curious pup, how I sometimes miss them. You would never have dreamed of interrupting my tales back then."

Malcolm had taken Nash under his wing when Nash had first started dabbling in the lifestyle. He'd always known he was a bit kinky and dominant in his needs. Malcolm had seen it as well but had taught him that to be a good Dom, one must understand what it was like to submit. Malcolm was the only man Nash had ever submitted to. Ever *would* submit to. "You're just bitter that I didn't give you more opportunity to spank my ass."

"So true." Malcolm sighed dramatically. "But back to current events. As I mentioned, Joshua has also agreed to the termination of his contract with Troy, but only if a new Dom is willing to take him on immediately."

"I'll take him." Nash surprised himself with how quickly he agreed to it. Then again, maybe it shouldn't be that surprising considering his feelings for the man.

"You will be wise to wait to make that decision until you have heard the full scope of the boy's issues. You haven't had a full-time sub in a very long time and to take one on such as Joshua will be an epic challenge."

"It's a no-brainer that I want him. Before taking him on full-time, I plan on learning everything there is to know about him, and we will ease into a more rigorous and strict agreement. I will set up a game plan for how to bring him back from the edge once I get to know him better." Nash was working on the logistics out loud as much for Malcolm's benefit as for his own.

"You're going to have to put your to-do lists and spreadsheets on the back burner. Joshua has nowhere to live, no money, no family to speak of—he's quite destitute. If you wish to have a relationship with Joshua, you will have to take him into your home immediately."

"Jesus, Malcolm! What the hell has this poor guy been through?"

"I don't know all the details. You will have to discover those for yourself if you agree to take him on. What I do know is, after the second time he had to be revived, his master abandoned him at the hospital here in Michigan and fled. His master went into hiding from what I understand. I can only assume the man feared being brought up on charges. Joshua had been his slave for nearly three years, but this…." Malcolm scowled, threw back his drink, and then wiped his hand across his mouth before he continued. "Barbarian left him with nothing and nowhere to go. Troy found him dirty and hungry, hustling for sex. So you see, as much as you dislike Troy, it is because of him that Joshua is no longer on the streets. He may very well have saved the boy's life."

Nash reached for his absent goatee again, but rather than drop his hand, this time he scrubbed his palm over his stubbled jaw. The situation was far worse than he'd imagined. The scars made sense now, and the way in which Joshua must have gotten them nauseated Nash. He swallowed down the bile that burned his throat and met Malcolm's concerned gaze. "This is too much. I don't know if I can handle it."

"It is a lot, but I know you, and if you take on this task, you will succeed."

Nash studied his friend and mentor for a moment. "Then why do you look so worried? Are you thinking the same thing I am?"

"Which is?"

"That Joshua may have been forced into the lifestyle and not joined by choice?"

"It has crossed my mind. You will have to learn that secret for yourself. I've arranged a dinner meeting with you and Joshua in"— Malcolm checked his watch—"thirty minutes."

"Talk about getting right to business," Nash grumbled, then looked down at his clothes. "I'm not dressed for dinner or to meet Joshua. I… I need more time."

Malcolm reached over and squeezed Nash's hand. "Would you like me to take the boy in? I can keep him safe until you've made your decision."

Nash wanted more time, his need to understand, to plan warring with his desire. Knowing what he did of Joshua's past, though, he couldn't stand the thought of passing him on to yet another temporary home. He hated being so unsure of himself, but he couldn't turn his back on Joshua. Nash shook his head. "No, I'll take him home with me," he finally told Malcolm.

"Are you sure?"

"No, but regardless, I'm still taking him."

Malcolm held Nash's gaze for a moment. Nash didn't blink. He might have been unsure, but he was determined to do what was right by Joshua. Malcolm must have seen it too, because he nodded, pushed out of his chair, and went to the closet. "I have a dinner jacket you can wear. Black or brown?"

Nash went and peered into the closet; it was full of different suits of various colors and patterns. "I guess black is more appropriate for this meeting."

Malcolm pulled one out and held it for Nash to shrug into it. Malcolm brushed his hands over the shoulders, then pulled Nash into a hug from behind. "I know you're worried about this and frankly, so am I. But I have complete confidence that if anyone can help this boy, it's you."

Nash hugged Malcolm's arms and leaned his head back against his friend's shoulder, taking some time to wrap his mind around all this new information. It wasn't taking Joshua on that he was hesitating over—Joshua going home with him was a given. Nash only wished he had more time to ease them both into the arrangement. "I'm glad I have your confidence. I'm going to need it since mine seems to be nowhere near as strong as yours."

"Then let me be your strength. I'm in this with you all the way."

Nash allowed Malcolm to hold his weight for a little longer, until his legs stopped shaking. He took a deep calming breath. "Thank you, my friend."

"Anytime." Malcolm briefly squeezed him tighter, then released Nash and stepped back. "All right, let's see what's on the menu for the night."

NASH SAT with his back against the dining room wall with an unobstructed view of the entrance. He'd taken the opportunity before Joshua arrived to, first, calm his frayed nerves and second, work out how to approach the topic of Joshua's past. Nash wouldn't jump into it right off the bat, but instead ease into it once Joshua had answered some easier questions. He wouldn't make the same mistakes he had the first night he'd spent with Joshua. Hopefully taking a casual approach would give him time to get to know the man a little better and understand what made him tick.

Although he was looking forward to seeing Joshua again—not only seeing him but taking him home—Nash wasn't only nervous, he was scared shitless in both his decision to take the sub on and in his ability to be what Joshua needed. All of it was unimportant the instant Joshua walked through the door.

Joshua was dressed in the same loose-fitting jeans and studded belt from the other night, but rather than the leather V, he wore a dingy white dress shirt. Nash stood as Denny led Joshua to his table.

"Good evening, Sir," Joshua greeted him, his eyes respectfully low.

"Good evening, Joshua, please have a seat."

Joshua pulled out the chair and sat, back ramrod straight, hands in his lap.

"Would you like something to drink?" Nash asked.

"Water is fine, Sir. Thank you."

Nash nodded to Denny. "Please bring Joshua some water and I'll have more tea."

Denny nodded and quickly moved away.

"While I appreciate your posture and manners, you are not here as my submissive and you do not have to avert your eyes. In fact, I'd appreciate being able to see them."

Joshua hesitantly raised his eyes, a shy smile curling his lips.

"That's better. You have beautiful eyes."

"Thank you, Sir. Yours are beautiful too. They remind me of coffee with a dash of cream."

"I've never heard them described quite like that. Usually, they are described as shit brown," Nash chuckled.

"They were wrong. There is nothing shitty about your eyes."

"Well, aren't we both full of compliments."

"Just pointing out a fact, Sir," Joshua said as Denny returned with their drinks.

Nash added a small amount of honey to his tea and stirred it without taking his gaze from Joshua. "I'd like to get a chance to talk to you before dinner is served if that's okay with you?"

"Yes, Sir. Whatever you would like is fine with me."

Nash nodded to Denny, who once again retreated. "It's Nash. You can call me by my given name."

"I mean no disrespect, but I'd prefer not to, Sir. It feels…. It's…." Joshua huffed out a breath. "It just doesn't feel right."

"It's okay, whatever you're comfortable with. I'm sure Malcolm has told you why you're here."

"Yes he has, Sir. Master Troy wants to terminate our contract and considering I agreed as long as he found me another Dom, I'm going to assume he turned to you."

"You're partially correct. I asked Malcolm to speak to Troy on my behalf. I've been quite intrigued by you for quite some time."

Joshua ran the tip of his finger over the droplets on his water glass. "I'm afraid once you learn more about me and my past, you might discover it was a waste of time."

"Your negotiation skills with a possible new Dom need a little work. Typically one talks about their attributes before their weaknesses."

"I'm not sure I have any," Joshua mumbled.

Joshua said it so quietly, Nash had to wonder if he'd been talking to himself. But Nash had heard him, and the sadness in Joshua's tone caused Nash's chest to tighten. It was Nash's job to prove the man wrong. He didn't believe it; he knew there was good in Joshua. Something had drawn him to Joshua, and Nash didn't doubt his gut.

"Okay, let's try this another way. How about I tell you little about me and what I am looking for," Nash suggested.

"I'd like that, Sir."

"I was born and raised right here in Flint. I just turned thirty-two this past May. I'm a huge art buff and even dabble in it a little with sketching and painting. I'm a financial advisor and work from home, but I am a bit of a workaholic. I've known that I was gay since I was ten or so and a kinkster after my first sexual experience at sixteen. Malcolm is my mentor, the first and last man I ever submitted to as I've always known I was dominant. I don't have a full-time sub, haven't in over three years, and even then, it was only for six months." Nash propped his elbow on the table and tapped a finger against his chin. "I have been a member of this club for nearly ten years and have earned the right to be respected. I'm a strict master and demand obedience. The one thing I will never, and I do mean never, tolerate is being lied to."

Nash sat back in his chair, taking his tea with him, and asked, "Anything else you need to know?" before taking a sip.

"Why me?"

"I'm not following you," Nash admitted.

"Why did you pick me? I mean, it sounds like you have your life together, Sir. Why would you want to get hooked up with a head case like me?"

Nash had to decide how much of himself to give away. The last thing he wanted to do was to let Joshua know he had doubts. He finally decided on part of the truth. "I was drawn to you from the first time I saw you. Honestly, I don't understand it completely, but I trust my gut, and it's telling me that you and I will make a good match."

Nash spotted Denny standing across the room waiting for Nash to call him when he was ready for dinner to be served. But Nash was no longer hungry and was ready to leave the club. Too many ears. Nash had no intention of making himself and Joshua the subject of gossip any more than they surely already were.

"Would you be terribly upset if we skipped dinner?"

"I'm okay with whatever you want, Sir." Joshua shrugged as if he didn't care either way, but Nash somehow got the feeling that Joshua was disappointed.

"I didn't mean eating. Only that I'd prefer to dine at home. Less of an audience to overhear our negotiations."

"I'd like that, Sir."

"Give me a minute to say good-bye to Malcolm and arrange for a car and we'll get out of here."

"Yes, Sir."

Nash pushed out of his chair and stood next to Joshua. He laid his hand on the man's shoulder and held his gaze. "I'm really glad you're here and will be coming home with me."

Chapter Four

NASH UNLOCKED the door and then pushed it open before stepping back. "After you."

Joshua walked into the foyer and whistled. "Holy shit! I mean, wow, you have a beautiful place, Sir." He started for the living room. "Nothing like I expected."

Nash closed the door and locked it before dropping his keys into the crystal bowl on the entryway table. "Thank you. Please remove your shoes."

"Oops, sorry." Joshua stepped back onto the tile floor and did as instructed. "For some reason, I had pictured you living in some fancy high-rise with chrome furniture and abstract works of art."

Nash couldn't help but notice how dingy Joshua's socks were or the large hole in the left one. He removed his boots and set them neatly on the rubber mat beneath the table. "I like the rustic charm of the cabin and the privacy it affords. Your socks too, please."

"Sure, no problem," Joshua responded easily, but the pink in his cheeks spoke of his embarrassment as he took off his socks and stuffed them into his battered boots.

"You'll find I can be quite difficult to live with. I'm a bit of a neat freak. I like everything tidy and in order."

"I think it's a Dom thing, Sir," Joshua pointed out as he continued to take in the room with an awed expression on his face. "I have learned it's not only their boys they like to control but their environment too."

Nash started to sit on the couch, then realized he still held a bag of Chinese takeout. He headed to the kitchen and set the food on the counter. He went to the cabinet, opened the door and closed it again and then did the same thing to the refrigerator. For some reason, he couldn't remember what he was supposed to be doing or even why he'd come into the kitchen. His mind was swimming with the events of the night. He had a full-time sub, for fuck's sake, and no real understanding of his new boy, no plan, nothing. He didn't even know what he was going to do in the next minute, let alone over the next six months.

"Do you mind if I use the bathroom, Sir? I'd like to wash up before I eat."

Nash spun around, startled, and stared at Joshua. "I'm sorry, what was that?"

"I asked if I could use your bathroom."

Nash gave himself an internal shake. *Fuck! Get it together, man.* "Sure, it's the only open door down the hall."

Joshua tilted his head, a concerned expression on his face. "Everything okay, Sir?"

"Yes, I'm all right. Don't mind me. It's been a long day. Go ahead and use the facilities and then we'll... umm." He spotted the takeout bag. "Then we'll have dinner."

Joshua continued to stare at him for a second and then turned and headed down the hall.

As soon as Joshua turned away, Nash let out a heavy sigh and threaded his fingers through his hair. He'd never been so off-balance before, and he didn't like the feeling one fucking bit. He had a job to do, a sub to take care of, but first he had to get a grasp on himself. He went to the sink and got a glass of water, gulping it down. Dry throat taken care of, Nash adjusted his clothes, rolled his neck, and then smoothed down his tousled hair. One of the things that made him successful in his career as a stock trader and financial advisor as well as a Dom was when he got frazzled, he didn't show it. He also recovered quickly.

"You got this." Nash nodded and straightened his shoulders. "You got this," he said once more, starting to believe it as the dizzying feeling began to ebb. When Joshua returned to the kitchen, Nash was back in control—or at least, that's what he told himself. *I got this.*

Nash smiled at Joshua and pointed toward the cupboard. "Would you mind getting some plates?"

As Joshua got the dishes, Nash grabbed silverware and brought it and the food to the table. "Have a seat. I'll get us something to drink. What would you like?"

"Water is fine, Sir."

When Nash returned to the table with two glasses of ice water, Joshua had the food out and was dishing it out. The tension in the man was obvious, and Nash decided his first priority was to set him at ease.

"I've told you a little about me, how about you tell me a little about you? Fair is fair," Nash said, keeping his tone light.

Joshua twirled his lo mein onto his fork. "You know I'm twenty-five, from Tennessee, and looking for a Dom. What else would you like to know, Sir?"

Nash remembered what Malcolm had told him about Joshua not having any family to speak of and knew he must not have had any kind of support system if he'd had to hustle the streets, so Nash steered away from asking any more questions about the man's early years, for now anyway. "How about what it is you're looking for in a Dom."

"Someone to serve, Sir."

"That's it?" Nash asked.

Joshua shrugged.

"Joshua, you have to give me something here. How about we try this another way. Tell me about your likes and dislikes."

"I like whatever it is my master likes, Sir."

Nash dropped his fork with a resounding clank. "Dammit, Joshua, I don't want an ass kisser, a slave, or a fucking robot. So if you want to be my submissive, I suggest you start opening your mouth and talk to me." *So much for keeping it light.* He apparently didn't have as much restraint or control as he'd hoped. Then again, with what he had learned about Joshua, perhaps being forward and stern worked better.

Joshua jerked back in the face of Nash's irritation, but he also sat straighter and lowered his eyes as his natural inclination to submit came to the forefront. Nash needed the truth from Joshua and if it took him being pushy, then so be it. How else could he help Joshua or find what they both needed?

"I'm sorry, Sir. I haven't been asked that question in a very long time. I'm usually told what I want and what I should feel," Joshua said.

A twinge of sadness settled into Nash. While he understood many submissives flourished under a strict routine, he had to wonder if that was actually the case with Joshua or if he simply knew no other way. "I'm asking you, and I need complete honesty from you. I know that it's going to be tough on you with a whole new set of rules and expectations. It's my job to see that you understand them and give you what you need. But I can't do that if I don't know what it is you're looking for and what it is you actually want out of our arrangement."

"I...." Joshua was silent for a long moment before he lifted his head and met Nash's gaze. "I want to belong. I want to stop feeling like I'm a fuckup, and I want to stop feeling like I don't matter."

Nash's sadness intensified. His heart ached with the sorrow obvious in Joshua's eyes. Nash's need to comfort was automatic and he reached across the table, laying his hand on Joshua's forearm. "Now we're getting somewhere. Tell me why you got into the lifestyle." While he was curious about Joshua's early years, home, family, all of it, he would discover them all along the way. He only needed to be patient.

"I always knew I was different even as a young teen. I liked to be tied up, spanked, I got off on being told what to do, ya know? A buddy of mine took me to a club one night, and I guess, as they say, the rest is history."

"And you stay why?"

Joshua cocked his head, looking at Nash as if he'd lost his mind. "I'm going to guess because of the same reason you do, Sir. The relationship between Dom and sub is intense and, with the right pairing, extremely pleasurable and rewarding."

"No offense, but the last time I saw you, it didn't look like you were having a great time."

"Yeah, I was having a hard time finding my headspace that night in the club, and you didn't help with that problem, Sir. And honestly, I've had a hard time focusing on much since. That kiss...." Joshua's smile was sweet, giving away some of what he'd thought about the simple act, but he didn't elaborate further.

While he was pleased the kiss had left an impact on Joshua, the rest of the evening he'd handled badly. However, he wasn't going to apologize again. He'd done what he'd thought was right at the time, and it had worked out since Joshua was now in his home discussing their possible future together.

Nash took a few minutes to enjoy his meal. The General Tso's chicken had just the right amount of spice, and the vegetable lo mein complemented it perfectly. He noticed Joshua was merely picking at his food. "Do you not like it? Would you prefer something else?"

Joshua jerked his head up. "Oh sorry, Sir. I was lost in thought for a moment. It's very good, Sir." He emphasized his statement by taking a large bite.

"What were you thinking about?" Nash asked, his interest piqued.

"Just trying to take it all in, ya know?"

"Meaning?"

"How I ended up here and what's going to happen next." Joshua shrugged as if he didn't care, but Nash knew better. The tension was written all over his handsome face.

"What's going to happen next is we are going to enjoy this lovely dinner," Nash told him with a wink.

"I like that plan, Sir." Joshua grinned, then took another bite of his dinner.

Once Nash had finished his last bite, he pushed his empty plate aside and sat back in his chair, taking his water glass with him. He sipped it while he thought about where to take the conversation. He decided not to comment on their previous interaction, instead keeping it in the present. "So let's get down to the root of why you're here. I don't like getting into a situation without having all the facts. It does neither of us any good. I understand you enjoy pain."

Again Joshua gave him that strange look, but this time, he chuckled. "Sure I do, but in a controlled sense. I mean, if you were to haul off and punch me in the face, I can't say I'd enjoy that too much. If it's controlled, allowed to build at a slow and steady pace? Oh yeah, I get off on it big-time. It can be a total rush."

Joshua's statement didn't surprise Nash, nor did the enthusiasm with which Joshua spoke of his like of pain. Nash already knew the answer to the next question but was curious as to how Joshua would answer, so he asked, "What about hard limits? Humiliation, water sports, or maybe blood play?"

Joshua shook his head. "If you need those things, then I wouldn't be opposed to any of them, Sir."

Nash took another sip of his water as he considered how to answer. That Joshua would allow such things was no shock, but that he agreed to such acts based on if his Dom required them was telling. Nash studied Joshua carefully. Did he really not mind such things or was it manipulation? Would he agree to anything as long as he got what he wanted in the long run? Nash would find the answer out as he spent more time with Joshua, he was sure. "I don't get off on nor will I subject you to any of those things. You said if *I* need them, but what about what you need?"

"Like I said—"

Nash held up his hand. "Remember, I don't want you to say what you think I want to hear or what you may have told others. I want the truth."

Joshua grinned shyly and averted his eyes, obviously still having a difficult time holding Nash's gaze. He chose instead to stare at his plate as he poked at the last of his noodles with his fork. "The truth is, I like it rough, very rough. But you already knew that, didn't you? I saw you talking to Kirk the other night."

"You see a lot with your head bowed. Of course I asked around about you. I'd have been a fool not to."

"And yet, here I am."

"I believe one of the first things we will work on is your confidence. That is, if you agree to my terms." Nash pushed up out of his chair. "I need more water. Would you like anything else?"

"No, thank you. I can get it for you, Sir."

"I'm already up." Nash went to the sink, feeling somewhat better. Joshua was still mostly an unknown, but he was starting to get a feel for him, and Nash liked the way it felt. They would play this Nash's way. Completely.

By the time Nash returned, Joshua had finished his meal. He wiped his mouth with the corners of his napkin and set it aside. "I'm ready to hear what you require of me, Sir."

Nash returned to his seat and grabbed a fortune cookie from the bag. He tossed it to Joshua, then took one for himself. Nash laughed when he read the small strip of paper within the cookie. *You're about to embark on a new journey.* Guess fortune cookies weren't always wrong. He nodded to Joshua, who was munching on his cookie while reading his fortune. "What's it say?"

"You're about to embark on a new journey."

That set Nash to laughing. "Okay, that's either really fucking creepy or someone ran out of good ideas." He tossed his fortune aside. "Mine says the same thing."

"Or maybe it's fate?"

"Hmm, could be," Nash agreed. A thought suddenly occurred to him. "I was thinking, you and I haven't done a scene together. Perhaps we should get a feel for one another, so to speak, before making any kind of commitment."

Joshua nodded but seemed disappointed by Nash's statement. "If you think it's necessary, Sir."

"You don't?"

"I know I like you and I can tell you're different from the Doms I've dealt with in the past." Joshua tilted his head up, looking at Nash from beneath his long, dark lashes. "Plus, you're not the only one who made inquiries. You have quite the reputation at the club."

Nash was glad to hear Joshua wasn't going into this blindly. Nash had assumed, perhaps incorrectly, that Joshua would have agreed to go with any Dom to get away from Troy. Joshua might not be as reckless as Nash had originally thought. Still, he knew the best way to understand how Joshua's mind worked was to get inside it.

"Let's get this table cleaned up and I'll show you how I earned that reputation."

Chapter Five

A TINGLING of excitement worked its way down Nash's spine as he led Joshua to his private playroom. For weeks, he'd fantasized about having Joshua here. Nash hadn't planned on all the other issues, but he was setting those aside for the time being. What he and Joshua needed was a chance to start at the beginning and find out how well they meshed in terms of their needs and desires.

Nash unlocked the door and crossed the room to the armoire. "Close the door behind you and then strip." He studied the contents of the cabinet as he considered his choices.

"Yes, Sir."

The sound of the door closing echoed around the room, and Nash turned to watch Joshua undress. He removed his shirt and started to drop it, but looked up at Nash and seemed to think better of it at the last second. Instead, he folded it and laid it neatly on the floor.

"You learn quickly," Nash praised.

"Thank you, I try, Sir."

Nash took a moment to appreciate Joshua's well-defined chest and muscular arms as he unfastened his belt and unbuttoned his jeans. When Joshua bent to pull off his pants, Nash was jolted back to reality when he spotted the scars that crisscrossed the man's back. It took considerable effort, but he was able to push down his anger and disgust at what had been inflicted upon Joshua. There would be time for exploring the rhyme and reason for those and to come to terms with them later, but not tonight.

Instead, Nash focused on Joshua's body as he stood and went to his display position. He hadn't taken the time to appreciate it when they'd been at the club, but he did so now. A spark of arousal warmed Nash, and his dick started to fill at the sight of Joshua's strong legs, muscular thighs, narrow hips, flat stomach, and half-erect cock. Joshua was in great shape, his body lean with well-defined muscles, a swimmer's build.

"Very nice," Nash hummed as he approached Joshua.

"Thank you, Sir. I'm glad you approve."

"Oh, I do." He brushed the tip of his finger over the head of Joshua's cock. "Some areas more than others."

He began to circle Joshua close enough to feel the heat of his body, but not close enough to touch. "What are your safewords?"

"I don't generally use them, Sir."

Nash stopped in front of Joshua. He took the man's chin in his palm and tilted his head up until their eyes met. "That is completely irresponsible as well as dangerous. You will use them with me or we won't play, is that understood?"

"Yes, Sir." Joshua swallowed hard as tension filled his frame. "Troy had me use *green, yellow,* and *red* as a reference to where I was at in a scene. I could use them if it's okay with you, Sir."

Nash would bet anything that Joshua never once used red, considering his past, but it was good to know Troy wasn't a complete idiot and didn't ignore safewords.

"You will use yellow if you wish me to slow down and red to stop. Is that understood?"

"Yes, Sir."

Nash released his hold on Joshua and began to walk slowly around him again. "I have no plans on pushing limits tonight, but even so, you should never play without safewords. Even a Dom you've put your trust in can make mistakes."

"I'll be sure to remember that, Sir."

"See that you do." Nash stopped at Joshua's back and leaned in to brush his lips against the man's ear. "Is it only pain you seek or pleasure?"

Joshua leaned his head back ever so slightly as a soft moan escaped his lips before he replied. "For me, they can be one and the same, Sir."

Nash licked the shell of Joshua's ear until he was rewarded with another moan. Nash slid his arm around Joshua's body and splayed his hand over his boy's chest. *My boy?* Oh, he did like the sound of that. "Can you have one without the other?"

"Very much so, Sir," Joshua moaned and took liberties by pressing his ass back against Nash's crotch, his meaning clear.

"And would you like to be fucked tonight?"

"God, yes, Sir."

"Then you must earn it by pleasing me. You do want to please me, don't you, boy?"

"Very much so, Sir."

Swaying his hips, Nash allowed Joshua to continue to rub against him, enjoying the pleasing sensation of his cock swelling until he was fully hard. "You have my permission to come whenever you want, as long as you don't deny me my pleasure." He kissed the side of Joshua's neck and spoke against his warm flesh. "But if you wait for me to ask it of you, you will find the rewards so much greater."

Joshua shifted a bit, leaning farther back against Nash, and tilted his head to give him more room to work. "I will wait for you, Sir."

"Good boy," Nash murmured, then kissed Joshua's neck one last time before releasing him to step back.

The playroom had an oversized leather couch covered with a multitude of pillows in golds, tans, and reds as well as a matching throw. With his previous full-time sub, he used this room not as a playroom but as a safe place where he and his boy could talk candidly as well as to deliver daily punishment and discipline. Nowadays he merely used it for an occasional scene, no longer using his basement playroom. Nash was looking forward to finding enjoyment within its walls again in the very near future.

"Get the pillows from the couch and arrange them in the center of the floor."

"Yes, Sir." Joshua went obediently to the sofa and brought back an armful of pillows. "How would you like me to arrange them, Sir?"

"You'll be on your hands and knees for quite some time, so however you feel they will be of best use to make you comfortable."

Nash unbuttoned the cuffs of his dress shirt and rolled up his sleeves as he watched Joshua arrange the pillows to his liking. He placed one for his head and one for his knees and piled the others in the center. Once he was finished, he stood and clasped his hands behind his back in a display position.

Joshua was now fully hard, his long, slender cock straining up toward his flat stomach. Nash enjoyed the sight of his boy's body for a moment longer. He liked the way Joshua's cock swayed with each breath and the flush of arousal working up his lean chest. He was quite a magnificent-looking man.

"Go to your hands and knees. Once you are in the position, you won't be allowed to move again, so I suggest you make yourself comfortable."

"Yes, Sir." Joshua knelt on one of the pillows and leaned over the pile, placing his hands on another one. The pillow slid and he pushed it aside, choosing instead to lay his hands flat on the floor.

"You are allowed to rest either your head or your elbows on the pillow if it makes you more comfortable," Nash informed him.

He turned away and walked to the armoire. He took a condom and a packet of lube and stuck them in the front pocket of his pants. He then studied the different types of crops and floggers he had. He had no intention of going back on his word. There would be no boundaries or limits pushed. However, knowing what he did of Joshua, the man would more than likely respond much better to the slap of a flogger than a gentle caress. Nash finally decided on a soft kangaroo flogger.

When he turned back around, Joshua had positioned himself with his arms folded on a pillow and his head resting upon them, his taut ass high in the air. When Nash walked to within Joshua's line of vision, his gaze went directly to the implement in Nash's hand and an audible sigh escaped him. Nash found the sound telling. While he didn't doubt Joshua was a sexual being, Nash had the sneaking suspicion that it would be difficult for him to achieve orgasm without an edge of pain. In fact, it was plausible that it could only be reached with substantial pain. Nash planned to find out.

"Are you comfortable?" Nash inquired.

"Yes, Sir." Joshua didn't take his eyes off the flogger.

Nash nodded. "Very good." He tested the weight of the flogger against his thigh. It had a nice snap to it but wouldn't cause Joshua any real pain, merely keep him focused. At least, that was the plan. He was delving into the unknown, but he hoped by going slow, only warming Joshua's skin, he'd be able to get Joshua to relax and find a good subspace. Maybe then Nash would get truly honest answers from his boy.

"I will be asking you a lot of questions; I want your honest answers. You may also beg, scream, and use any words or sounds you wish. Your mind is your own, but your body is mine. You will not move or hinder my movements in any way. Is that understood?"

"Yes, Sir. I understand," Joshua responded without hesitation. His skin flushed a lovely shade of pink, the color working up from his ass to his neck. The anticipation and excitement in his boy was evident.

Nash tested the weight of the flogger against his own thigh again with a little more strength. He'd chosen one with a long handle so he wouldn't have to bend as he worked Joshua's flesh. He could sustain the blows easily for a long time without worrying about getting sore or exhausted. Something necessary, he was sure, since it would no doubt take time to work Joshua up to a state in which Nash could assure honesty in his answers.

Satisfied with his choice, Nash ran the soft tails along Joshua's spine, down to his ass cheeks and thighs, before moving back up. "Very well, we begin." That was all the warning he gave Joshua before he flicked his wrist, putting just enough weight behind it that Joshua would feel the slap but no pain.

The hurt would come from the sheer number of blows. A slow buildup so Nash could evaluate each change in Joshua with ease. He needed to know how well Joshua dealt with restrictions on his movement, how much pain was required before Nash got a reaction, the way the man processed it. This was a chance to discover some of Joshua's secrets, truthful ones, ones he couldn't hide behind pretty words and learned, respectful answers.

"What is it you hope to achieve?" Nash laid another slap on Joshua's back.

"Peace," Joshua answered without hesitation.

"Interesting response," Nash said. "When is the last time you experienced peace?"

"I don't know that I ever have, Sir." Other than Joshua's skin turning a nice rosy shade, there was no other indication that he felt the blows.

Nash continued to lay down slaps, keeping a steady rhythm and giving away no indication of how Joshua's response had affected him.

To have never felt peace? Nash's first response was sadness, but then it occurred to him that perhaps Joshua was giving what he thought was the expected answer. Nash found it even sadder that he didn't trust Joshua had given him an honest answer.

"Do you mean as an adult?" Nash asked, trying to clarify Joshua's meaning.

"Yes, Sir, and as a child too," Joshua responded, sounding sincere.

Nash once again nearly stuttered in his movements as his chest tightened. Dammit, Joshua was either being honest or a master manipulator. Nash hated that he didn't know which. He continued to swing the flogger, letting it fall over and over until the sound of the leather against skin soothed Nash. Only after he had calmed himself down was he able to continue asking questions.

"Yet I suspect you find peace in pain."

"Yes, Sir, or I used to think I did, but I'm not even sure that I actually ever achieved it. Maybe it's oblivion I'm seeking rather than peace."

With that response, Nash forced himself to keep swinging, although his first inclination was to drop the damn flogger and take Joshua into his arms. To deny Joshua pain now wouldn't help either of them. Nash was sure if he withheld it, Joshua would only act out or, worse, run. The thought of Joshua seeking out another Dom, one who wouldn't know when to quit, made Nash nauseated.

Although Nash wasn't 100 percent confident in his abilities, he didn't let on. Instead, he kept his voice and his arm steady when he responded, "I can help you find peace, but oblivion can only be truly experienced in death. Do you have a death wish, boy?"

"I—" Joshua's words were cut off by a slap of the flogger to his lower back. Nash made a mental note of the location and moved back up to Joshua's shoulders. "I don't believe I do, Sir," Joshua finally admitted.

"That's not an outright denial, which causes me a great deal of concern."

"I have no plans to off myself. I almost said no, but you wanted complete honesty."

"I won't stand for anything less," Nash said with conviction.

"Yes, Sir. I understand that. It's why I answered the way I did. I'm a bit of an adrenaline junkie, have been since I was a kid." Joshua sucked in a harsh breath. He arched his back briefly when another well-placed blow landed in another sensitive spot, directly between his shoulder blades. He blew out a breath and relaxed before continuing. "I suppose with that there is always the risk of being hurt or even killed."

"An adrenaline junkie, huh?"

"Yes, Sir. I love fast cars and even faster motorcycles. I've crashed both, broke my leg on a bike when I was sixteen, yet I still have a lead foot. I don't know, I guess what some call a death wish, I call crazy ass fun. That's why I answered the way I did."

Nash hadn't expected such a thoughtful response, but that Joshua had put so much consideration into Nash's question pleased him to no end. "Ah, remind me never to let you drive."

"Yes, Sir," Joshua said, the amusement in his tone evident.

Nash smiled. He let the flogger fall for a few moments, enjoying the rhythmic sound and the sight of Joshua's glowing flesh. The man had settled back easily into a relaxed position, not giving any outward appearance that he felt the blows. Only then did Nash realize he was avoiding Joshua's sensitive areas as well as the scars. He started to ask about them, but once again changed his mind. He would, but the time had to be right. Perhaps he would address them once Joshua was in his arms so Nash could easily bring comfort.

"You said you were a teenager when you realized you had a penchant for pain and submission, but tell me about the first time you were with a true Dom."

"I was eighteen and went to a club. I volunteered for a stage show that involved a public flogging. I was pretty much hooked from that moment on."

"Had you ever been flogged before?"

"No, Sir."

Nash spread his blows out without ignoring the places that made Joshua groan or twitch as well as moving down to the untouched skin of Joshua's ass. Nash was rewarded with a sharp gasp of breath and the first evidence of tension in Joshua's body. "Were his blows as light and steady as mine?"

"No, you have a very fine hand, Sir. My first experience with a Dom left me bleeding and in tears."

"And yet you say you were hooked."

"Yes, Sir. I think it may have something to do with my stubborn nature. Or maybe it was my love of the adrenaline rush that had me hooked. Whatever the reason and while I was sore as hell, I was bound and determined to withstand the pain like I'd witnessed other subs do."

Joshua's addiction to pain was beginning to make sense. Seeing as Joshua got off on the "rush," it was no wonder he was always looking for the bigger and better high. Unfortunately, his past experiences were with Doms who either didn't understand that or didn't care. A high, whether from drugs, alcohol or pain, had to be experienced in moderation or the consequences would be an unhealthy addiction. It would be up to Nash to be mindful of Joshua's natural tendency to submit while giving him the pain he craved in a healthier way than he had had in the past.

When Nash concentrated his blows on Joshua's ass and upper thighs, Joshua's breath caught and he moaned, the sound laced with arousal. Joshua had already been hard before he went to his knees, although that was more than likely due to anticipation than anything else. Now he was definitely responding to the steady stinging blows. Nash added slightly more weight to the flogger, and from that moment, every slap and sting seemed to register more acutely with Joshua. His back would arch to meet one lash of the flogger, shy away from another. It was like a dance between the two of them, the slap of the flogger against flesh the melody. The movements and sounds were hypnotic, and Nash lost himself in it for several moments.

Only once Nash was in a good headspace and he believed Joshua was as well did he speak again. "You said your first experience was a public flogging. How long after did you enter into your first contract with a Dom?"

"Within six months, I'd say." Joshua's voice was tight, as if he were having a difficult time formulating words. His moans, however, were quite lovely and flowed from him with ease.

"And did you complete the contract successfully?"

"No, Sir."

Nash kept his arm steady, working Joshua's flesh from shoulder to thigh, waiting for Joshua to expand on his answer. When he didn't add anything further, Nash prompted him. "Did you get what you needed out of the arrangement?"

"I didn't think so at the time. It was frustrating. I…. Ah, damn." Joshua arched his back, body going bowstring tight when a well-placed slap hit his balls. His eyes squeezed shut, Joshua blew out several heavy breaths before he settled back into a relaxed position. "We didn't work out, but I did learn a lot about submitting and putting another person's needs before my own."

"Hmm. I can see why it didn't work out. While you should always make your Dom the object of your focus, you cannot ignore your needs. They should be met through him."

"I have very few needs, Sir."

Joshua's skin was turning a deeper shade of red, causing the stark white scars to stand out in contrast. It wasn't only the way Joshua's flesh was responding to the constant blows, but the way the man himself was responding. Other than the slap to his balls, Joshua seemed to have somehow shut the pain out. He was no longer moaning or swaying with the blows but completely still and without any evidence of tension in his muscles. "And which is the most important to you?" Nash asked, curious if Joshua would respond by saying it was pain. But he didn't.

"Food and shelter, I suppose."

"You suppose?"

"Yes, Sir. I mean, I have other wants and desires, but they are the only real needs I have."

Nash's arm began to ache, and he switched hands, keeping his rhythm steady and even. He ran a critical eye over Joshua's flesh. He found no evidence of any broken skin or abrasions. Even though Joshua had hit a plateau, Nash refused to put more weight behind his swings. "For the preservation of your physical being, but what about what you need to keep your mind healthy?"

"I need to please my master."

"Must I remind you I want the truth?"

"Yes, Sir, I remember. I wasn't just saying it. I honestly believe it. If I can please my master, then he is happy and, in turn, will reward me and make me happy. And isn't that what all of us want? Happiness?"

"And when was the last time you had a truly happy master?"

"Well…." Joshua didn't continue for a few ticks of the clock while he shifted his position slightly, the pillow beneath his knees beginning to slide. The silence drew out even after Joshua stilled. Nash was about to encourage him to continue when he said, "I'm not very good at pleasing people."

"That's not what I asked."

Joshua let out an audible sigh. "It's the answer I'm giving, Sir."

They were at an impasse. Joshua was no longer able to maintain his subspace and Nash wasn't willing to increase the level of pain. He slowed his movements, at the same time easing up on the weight of each blow. He ran the strands of leather gently along Joshua's spine from the base of his neck to his ass and then walked back to the armoire. He returned the flogger and shook out his arms. Joshua might not be satisfied with the flogging, but Nash was happy with the results. He'd learned much about Joshua through his actions, but he'd learned even more through his reactions.

"Stand and display."

Joshua quickly moved into the position Nash instructed, a deep frown marring his brow. Nash kept his steps deliberate and measured as he strolled back to Joshua. He came to a halt behind him and inspected Joshua's reddened flesh again. He nodded when satisfied there was no broken skin. Joshua hissed when Nash laid his hands against Joshua's back. He took a moment to enjoy the heat his marks produced.

"Your back is quite lovely."

"It feels good too, Sir. I wouldn't mind experiencing more of your talented wielding of the flogger."

Nash slid his arms around Joshua and pulled him close, smiling when he was rewarded with another hiss. "But this is about my pleasure," he whispered against Joshua's ear. He soaked in Joshua's heat and enjoyed the feeling of the smooth skin of Joshua's chest against his palms. "I do believe you said one of your main needs was to please your master. Do you hope for me to master you?"

"Yes, Sir."

"Good." Nash released Joshua and stepped back. "Put your clothes on and join me in the living room."

Nash bit down on his lip to keep from laughing at the frustrated sound that came from Joshua. Luckily he'd left the room and was out of earshot when the snort of amusement escaped him. Joshua might beg to differ, but Nash thought their first experience together had been quite successful. A plan on how to deal with Joshua and his needs was quickly forming.

Chapter Six

JOSHUA STARED, stunned, at the empty doorway long after Nash disappeared, trying to figure out what the hell had just happened. Sure, he'd had men hit him lightly as a warm-up, but it always escalated. Always. Not only did the blows get more intense but also nearly every time it ended with Joshua having a dick either up his ass or down his throat. Sometimes both.

He grabbed his jeans and shirt from the floor and slid them on. His head swam with the turn of events. He'd known Nash was unlike anyone he'd ever met after the night Nash had taken him to the back room of the Underground. But this….

This made no sense.

Doms wanted one thing. Power. Sure, they got off on telling someone what to do, showing their superiority over another person, but it was always about *their* pleasure, *their* orgasm, and *their* needs. Oh, they used pretty little words to assure their submissive that through their pleasure, he would be rewarded. Joshua used to believe it. He no longer did. Everything about the lifestyle had thrilled him when he was a teenager. But he soon discovered black leather covered not only bodies but intent as well. He had yet to meet one Dom who wasn't on a major power trip. Which was fine by him. More power to them was his motto. They could boss him around all they wanted, could have multiple orgasms for all he fucking cared, as long as he got his three Ps: pleasure, pain, and peace. Regardless of what he'd told Nash, there was peace in pain. He'd experienced it a couple of times. The sensation was unlike anything he'd experienced, a euphoria he'd been chasing ever since and had yet to find.

If this was Nash's idea of domination, he had a lot to learn, and Joshua was the perfect sub to teach him how to really take control. There was so much more to it than a little slap and tickle. *And no orgasm?* Joshua shook his head. *Weirdo.* He buttoned up his shirt and went to join Nash.

He found Nash in the kitchen putting leftover Chinese in plastic containers. He turned and smiled at Joshua. "There is some disinfectant and a rag under the sink. You can wipe off the table and the counters while I finish up here."

"Yes, Sir." Joshua grabbed what he needed and did as he was told.

He had so many questions to ask and comments to make, but he kept his mouth shut. It was a game, one he had thought he'd mastered. Since that night when the erotic asphyxiation scene went horribly wrong and Corbin bolted, however, Joshua had been struggling. He wasn't about to screw this new arrangement up with his loose tongue. He would get what he wanted from Nash one way or another.

"All done." Joshua held up the cleaner and cloth.

"You can put the cloth in the hamper." Nash nodded to a closed door.

Joshua returned the cleaner to its place and then opened the door Nash had indicated. It was a bathroom. Everything in it, tub, toilet, sink, lights, walls, and even the hamper, was bright white. *This is going to be a bitch to keep clean*, he surmised and dumped the cloth in the hamper. Bright whites, disinfectants, no shoes in the house? He was definitely going to have to step up his Susie Homemaker skills.

"I'm going to put on a pot of coffee. Would you like some?" Nash offered.

"I'm not much of a coffee drinker, Sir."

"Ah, stick with me and I'll make a coffee snob out of you for sure." Nash opened the cupboard above the coffeemaker to reveal dozens of the little tin containers. He studied them for a moment and then grabbed one that had Kenya Nyeri printed on it. He poured the beans into a grinder and then added the grinds to the coffee machine.

"You can't get coffee in the supermarket! That stuff is just wrong," Nash said, his tone light and easy like he hadn't just left Joshua hanging. "I mean, I guess it's fine if you just want a caffeine buzz to start the morning. To really enjoy the experience, though, you need a good blend from either Kenya or Ethiopia. Then there is my personal favorite, Panama La Esmeralda. I only have it for special occasions. At sixty-two dollars for eight ounces, I can't justify the price on a daily basis."

As Nash moved around the kitchen preparing his coffee and rambling on and on, Joshua stared at him in utter shock. Was he not going to mention what happened in the other room? Was he not going to apologize for not finishing his fucking job? Joshua pressed his lower back against the corner of the cupboard, letting the spark of pain help get his racing thoughts under control before he ended up blurting them out. *Play the game.*

Once Nash had his coffee, he grabbed a pad of paper and a pen and had Joshua join him at the dining room table. He didn't say anything for a long while, tapping his pen against the table and sipping his coffee while staring out the window. Each tick of the clock had Joshua's tension ratcheting up until he felt like an overwound toy about to pop its springs and bolts.

Just when Joshua thought he couldn't stand the silence a second longer, Nash turned his head and met Joshua's gaze. "I think tonight was a good start. Mind you, it was merely a small test, but I think you and I could work nicely together. How about you?"

"Yes, Sir, I agree. It was most satisfying," Joshua was able to get out, keeping his tone even.

Joshua jerked when Nash burst out laughing.

"What's so funny, Sir?"

"I'm just pleased with myself is all," Nash sniffed. "I suspected you would say that even though you know damn good and well I was the only one satisfied."

"That's all that matters, Sir," Joshua replied without hesitation.

Nash narrowed his eyes. Joshua didn't flinch or look away. After a tense moment, Nash said, "Yes, well, we shall see." He slid the pen and paper across the table. "What I'd like for you to do is spend a little time writing out your likes and dislikes."

Joshua picked up the pen and nodded. "Yes, Sir."

"Good, I'll be back in a half hour." And with that, Nash took his coffee and left the room.

Joshua picked up the pen, chewing on the end of it as he considered the blank page before him. *A small test, huh?* He was sure this was another one. Of course, his first thought was to write the standard likes. Submitting, pleasing his master, and of course, being fucked. While the last one was true, it wasn't at the top of his list. But if he did put what he liked most at the top, would Nash deny him the pain he so craved? Doms were always withholding things from their submissives as punishment or to prove some fucking point.

He tossed around what to write, but after twenty minutes, he'd done little more than draw out two columns and numbered one through ten under each of the headings. Part of him wanted to be completely honest with Nash. But what the hell had his honesty gotten him so far? A whole lot of heartache, that's what it had fucking gotten him. Screw it, he knew he was a damn good submissive, and he did need a place to stay.

He started scribbling down his answers.

NASH STROLLED into the dining room, ignoring the expectant expression on Joshua's face. He went and poured another cup of coffee, glancing at the clock. He had two more minutes, even though he knew from the pen sitting next to the paper that Joshua was done. He held up the pot. "You sure you don't want a cup? Or something else to drink?"

"No thank you, Sir."

"Suit yourself." Nash slid into the chair opposite Joshua. "Are you finished?"

Joshua slid the pad across the table. "Yes, Sir."

Nash turned the paper around and studied it while he sipped his coffee.

Favorites:

Crops

Bullwhip

Paddles

Cock and Ball Torture

Breath play.

"I see some of your favorites are a little extreme. I am not a fan of the bullwhip, but I'm quite skilled with it. You will have to work hard to earn that privilege."

Joshua's smile was genuine. "I'll try my hardest to earn it, Sir."

"I'm sure you will." Nash turned his attention back to the list, nodding at several of the items. He found it interesting that Joshua's dislikes were less harsh than the things he liked. The kangaroo flogger and feathers didn't surprise Nash, but the total sensory deprivation, as well as a few others, did.

"I find your list a bit confusing. What is it about the electrical shock that scares you?"

"I don't know that it scares me so much as it…." Joshua frowned, then shrugged. "I don't like the sensation. It feels like bugs crawling on me, which kind of freaks me out."

"And total sensory dep?" Nash inquired.

"I actually used to enjoy it, but then I had a bad experience with it," Joshua said calmly. "I guess if I found the right Dom, one I could trust unconditionally, I would allow it again. There really isn't much I won't do. Blood and breath play are major turn-ons." Joshua lowered his head, suddenly very interested in the hangnail on his thumb he'd been picking at. "I know you talked to Kirk, and I'm sure he told you about my, um, pain tolerance."

"He mentioned it," Nash said evenly. There was no sense in lying to Joshua or pretending it wasn't going to be an issue. Nash believed in putting his cards on the table and having a prospective sub do so as well. He already had the feeling that Joshua would hold back or sugarcoat his extreme needs. "In fact, you frightened him a bit. Kirk is a harsh master and rattling him is very difficult."

"We didn't mesh," Joshua responded flippantly.

Nash was looking forward to starting this journey with Joshua, but this arrangement was about much more than his own needs, but Joshua's as well. Nash was no fool. He had no unrealistic notions that it would be easy. But with patience, complete honesty, and a firm hand they might have a shot at satisfying those needs. He couldn't forget, however, that Joshua would more than likely try to manipulate him to achieve his own goals.

Normally Nash was confident that he could control most situations. Even though Joshua had shaken him, he was determined. If he didn't think he could handle it, he sure as hell wouldn't be taking the man on.

He tore the list from the pad and folded it carefully, then stuck it in his shirt pocket before he stood. "It's been a long day. I'll show you where you will be sleeping."

"That's it?"

"Meaning?" Nash tossed over his shoulder as he led the way from the room.

"I don't know; I thought we would be discussing contracts."

Nash stopped outside the spare bedroom, hand poised over the knob. "There is no hurry. I thought it best we both have a chance to ponder what we've talked about so far and get a good night's rest. We can discuss something as important as a contract in the morning." He opened the door and ushered Joshua in. "This will be your room." He pointed to one of the closed doors. "That is the bathroom. Go ahead and take a shower, there are towels beneath the sink. I'll be right back."

"Sir? Where are you going?"

The slightly panicked tone in Joshua's voice had Nash stopping at the door. "I'm just going to go get you some clean clothes to put on."

"Oh, okay. Thank you, Sir."

Nash watched Joshua as he took in the room, running his fingers over the bed and across the dresser, looking confused and a little lost. "Joshua?"

"Yes, Sir?" Joshua met Nash's gaze.

"It really has been a great night, and I'm glad you're here."

Joshua worried his bottom lip with his teeth. "I'm happy to be here."

Nash left the room unsure if Joshua was being truthful and knew pain was only one of the issues they would have to work through. But first, Nash had to earn his trust.

Chapter Seven

NASH FOUND himself wide awake long before the first rays of morning snuck through the pulled curtains. Not yet willing to get up, he ran through each and every detail of the night before and began to formulate a plan. He still wasn't sure he could be what Joshua needed. What he did know was he was going to bust his balls to make it work.

They needed a schedule. Joshua would need to be kept busy and feel useful. Given the man's past, Nash figured it would take time for Joshua to settle into his life here. Only then, once Joshua knew Nash wasn't going to pass him around or abandon him, could they work on the core of Joshua's issues.

But first they were going to have to agree to contract terms and deal with the legalities first.

It was Nash's bladder that finally forced him from his bed far sooner than he was ready. A quick piss, a shower, and a brush of his teeth, and he headed for the kitchen. Eventually, he would expect Joshua to be out of bed and have the coffee made before Nash got up. *Out of my bed.* The thought made him smile, and he whistled while he set the coffee to brew.

"Good morning, Sir."

Nash turned around to find Joshua standing in the doorway to the kitchen with a sleepy smile on his face in nothing but a pair of loose sweatpants.

"Good morning. Did you sleep well?"

"No, Sir."

"I'm sorry. Was there something wrong with the bed?"

"No, it was great, very comfortable. I'm just not used to sleeping alone and I couldn't find the off switch in this crazy brain of mine." Joshua rapped his knuckles against his head.

"How about you come help me make breakfast and we can discuss your crazy?"

"Yes, Sir. I'm pretty handy in the kitchen."

Nash turned and leaned against the counter. "Really?"

"Yes, Sir, Master Corbin insisted that I make all his favorites quickly and efficiently. His taste changed from week to week, so...." Joshua shrugged and pulled open the fridge. "What would you like for breakfast, Sir?"

Master Corbin, huh? That was one man Nash planned on finding and having a bit of a chat with. "I was going to make a couple of simple omelets and toast, but how about you surprise me with your culinary skills?"

Joshua studied the contents of the fridge for a moment longer and then started pulling out items and setting them on the counter. "If you'll point me in the direction of the pots and pans and some cooking utensils, I'll get started."

"Go ahead and take a minute to get acquainted with the kitchen. I need to do some caffeinating." Nash grabbed a mug from the cupboard and filled it with coffee. He inhaled the rich brew, then took a tentative sip, the flavor even better than the scent. He took another sip and held up his mug. "I don't know how you can't be a fan of this."

Joshua halted his exploration of the kitchen long enough to look back at Nash over his shoulder and wrinkled his nose. "I guess it's an acquired taste."

"Yes, kind of like wine. I hated them both the first time I tried them."

Joshua pulled out a cutting board from the lower shelf and set it on the counter. He grabbed a knife from the block and started cutting up vegetables. "I don't get that, Sir. If you didn't like them the first time, why in the world would you keep drinking them?"

Nash took a seat at the island and wrapped his hands around his mug. "Hmm, good point. The coffee was a must-have in college and the wine...." Nash tapped his fingers against the mug as he tried to remember why in the hell he started drinking wine. *Oh yes. Toby.* The one time in his life he'd thought he was in love and was trying to impress. He'd soon discovered it wasn't about hearts and flowers and was more about his dick. "The wine was all about getting laid."

"I guess there are worse things to put in your mouth to get a little dick." Joshua snickered.

True to his word, Joshua was handy in the kitchen. Once he knew where everything was, he moved around the room easily, cutting up vegetables, whipping eggs, flipping hash browns, and toasting bread. Nash enjoyed the scents wafting up but enjoyed the sights even more. Joshua was naturally an extremely handsome man, but when he was relaxed and confident, he shined.

Nash downed the last of his coffee, and before he could even set his mug back down, Joshua was there to refill it. "Very observant," Nash praised, tickled to no end.

"I try, Sir. Breakfast is about ready. Would you like me to serve it here or in the dining room?"

"Here is fine."

Joshua set out napkins and silverware as well as two glasses of ice water and juice before returning to the stove and filling their plates. The first one he set down in front of Nash was filled with a thick omelet covered in what appeared to be salsa. A second plate contained ham steaks and hash browns and a third had toast.

"Wow. This looks and smells amazing," Nash complimented. "I hope you plan on helping me eat this."

"Nope, that's all yours. I only hope it tastes as good as it looks." Joshua sat on the stool next to Nash with a single plate of food.

Nash looked at the small amount of food Joshua had on his plate and then arched a brow. "I think someone is trying to fatten me up."

"I wasn't sure how much you normally eat, so I figured giving you too much was better than not enough."

Nash bumped his shoulder against Joshua's. "That was very thoughtful of you."

"Thank you, Sir." Joshua folded his hands in his lap, his cheeks turning a cute shade of pink with the praise.

Nash studied him for a moment, pleased that Joshua didn't pick up his fork until Nash tried the eggs. They were light, fluffy, and full of flavor, and he hummed his approval. "These don't only smell and look good, they taste amazing."

"Thank you, Sir. If you'll give me a list of your favorite foods, I'll be sure to add them to the menu. I don't mean to overstep my bounds, but I assume I'll be doing the cooking and cleaning."

Nash took another bite. "Oh yes, you definitely have the job of chef around here." He washed down the eggs with a sip of coffee before continuing. "I guess we should talk about what would be expected of you as my full-time submissive, as long as you don't mind me talking while I eat."

"I don't mind, Sir. I get a little twitchy when I don't know what I'm supposed to be doing."

"Can I ask you a personal question before we begin?"

"Of course, Sir. You can ask me anything."

"Malcolm has told me you have no money and nowhere to live. If you did…. Let's say you had plenty of money, would you still be looking for a full-time Dom?"

Nash was pleased when Joshua didn't answer right away. Instead, he continued to chew his food slowly with a thoughtful expression on his face. Nash didn't push, giving him all the time he needed to consider the question. Plus, the breakfast really was amazing, and he happily munched on it.

It was several minutes before Joshua finally answered. "I think I would have a bit more confidence, probably wouldn't feel like such a loser if I had my own money. But…." He nodded, his expression turning to determination. "Yeah, I would still want to be in a full-time Dom/sub relationship. Don't get me wrong, there was a time I might not have answered that the same way. I hit some pretty low moments in my life, and I'm still trying to come to terms with those things. But…. Yeah, even if I had money, I would still want this. My submission, or rather, my need to submit, has been a part of me since I was a youngster. It was part of me before the bad things happened, and for some reason, it still is."

Joshua looked up from his plate and met Nash's gaze questioningly. "Does that make me a freak or just stupid?"

"It makes you neither," Nash assured him. "Your need to submit is part of your nature, and there is nothing wrong with it or you. Which leads us back to the business at hand." Nash finished the last bite of his breakfast, wiped his mouth on his napkin, and then pushed it and his empty plate aside.

Nash waited until Joshua set his fork down and turned to face him before he continued. "As my submissive you really only have one rule—to please me. That means always thinking about my needs before your own and knowing that I will fulfill yours. There will be daily chores. As you already know, I'm a little compulsive when it comes to cleanliness and organization. I'll be sure to supply you with any products you need to do your job. If there is something that will make your job more efficient, you only have to ask. Notice I did not say easier. I'm obviously not going to hire you a maid to do it for you."

"No, I didn't suspect you would, Sir." Joshua chuckled.

Nash took a sip of his coffee. The lukewarm temperature made him wrinkle his nose, and he went to pour another cup.

"You'll also be cooking all the meals. I'm not a fan of frequent trips to the store. I'll take you once a week, so be sure you have a proper list or you'll have to improvise. Other than chores, there will be daily discipline each morning, and any punishment strikes you earn will be administered before bed." He turned to lean against the counter and looked Joshua in the eye. "Any questions or problems so far?"

"No, Sir." Joshua gestured toward the dirty dishes. "Would you mind if I cleaned up the breakfast mess while we continue to chat?"

"Not at all." Nash thrummed his fingers on the counter. "Where was I? Oh yes, nightly punishment," he said, answering his own question before Joshua had a chance. "You'll go to bed when I do, and you'll sleep in your own room. You will have the opportunity to earn the right to sleep in my bed. I'm an early riser, so if you're not, you'll have to set an alarm. I like to start my day with coffee, and I get cranky if I am denied it. Trust me, you won't like me if I am not well caffeinated in the morning."

"I'll be sure to have it ready, Sir."

"Smart boy," Nash praised. He thought about what else he should tell Joshua while the boy did the dishes. Nash was pretty simple in his needs. Coffee, food, clean house, and pleasure. Joshua bent to retrieve the dishcloth he dropped, putting his pert little butt on display. Nash smiled. *Lots and lots of pleasure.*

"That's all I can think of at the moment. The rest we'll figure out as we go along, I suppose. Any questions?"

"Just one, Sir. And forgive me for asking this again, but why me?"

"Why not you?" Nash countered. "Are you saying you won't be able to do what is expected of you?"

Joshua dried his hands and set the towel aside. He turned toward Nash but kept his eyes lowered. "No, I'm sure I can, it's just…. Well…." Joshua stayed silent for several ticks of the clock before he huffed out a heavy breath. "I guess I shouldn't look a gift horse in the mouth. I'm sorry for asking, Sir."

"It is still to be determined if I'm a gift," Nash teased, doing his best to lessen some of the tension that had settled upon Joshua.

Joshua snapped his head up and met Nash's gaze. "You already are. I admit I'm having a hard time figuring you out. You're not like anyone I've ever met. But I like you. A lot. And your home." Once again Joshua averted his eyes and shifted from foot to foot. "I don't have any money, so I can't pay for my room and board."

"I don't expect any money from you. Trust me, you will earn your keep. If you'd like to seek outside employment, I won't stop you. However, seeing as I work from home, I'd prefer you to be here to take care of me."

"I would rather be here as well, Sir."

"Good, then it's settled." Nash set his mug down and slung his arm over Joshua's shoulder. "C'mon, I'll give you a tour of the rest of the house and then we'll talk contract."

He led Joshua past the areas he was already familiar with, the kitchen, living room, down the hall past his room and the temporary playroom, which Nash now planned to use as a safe room. A place where they could discuss issues, give discipline and perhaps even his punishment. He'd crack the door on his basement playroom and only use the safe room as a place to talk. An area where they could drop their roles as Dom and sub so Joshua would have an opportunity to speak freely. So many things to think about, plan, organize. *One thing at a time*, he reminded himself. Tour, contract, and then there would be plenty of time for figuring out the rest.

Nash opened the door next to his master suite and ushered Joshua in. "This is the laundry room. I know it may seem like a strange place for it, but I'm all about efficiency." He pointed to the door to the left. "That leads directly to my closet."

Joshua took in the room, running his hand down the stainless steel counter with the ironing board built in. "Wow, this is nicer than a lot of the bedrooms I've been in. Fancier too."

Nash looked around the room. It was far from fancy. Sure, it had high-tech appliances, organized shelves, sorting bins, etc. He'd designed it for productivity with the fewest number of steps. If Joshua thought this was impressive, he was really going to be wowed by Nash's office. He couldn't help but puff up a little with pride that Joshua liked his home. A home that, hopefully soon, Joshua would come to believe was his as well.

"C'mon, let me show you the rest of the place."

Chapter Eight

THE HOUSE was beyond Joshua's wildest dreams. He'd never stayed at such a nice place before. Troy's house had been okay, but he didn't care about decorating, and his small ranch-style house hadn't been updated since he'd bought it over two decades before. The one thing that Troy did spend money on was his playrooms—plural. Troy was all about being the top dog, and he never faltered or fell out of his role as Dom. Nash, on the other hand, was completely different. Easy to talk to, almost sweet, and so fucking caring, Joshua couldn't help but be suspicious. He'd dealt with a lot of Doms, and Nash was in a league of his own. The workshop he stepped into was more proof of how unusual and complex Nash was.

The walls were covered with brightly colored landscapes and abstract paintings. Rags, paint cans, brushes, and coffee mugs were scattered around the multiple counters and tables. The scent of paint, varnish, and linseed oil was heavy in the air. Where Nash's house was clean and organized, the workshop was pure chaos.

"Do you rent out the workshop?" Joshua inquired.

"No, why?" Nash obviously picked up on Joshua's amazement because he gestured around the room. "Oh, you mean how crazy messy it is. It's the one place I can come and let go of everything. My creative side isn't real big into organization, but don't worry, I don't expect you to keep this room clean."

Joshua picked up a mug. The bottom was covered in a dark black sludge and looked as if it had been sitting there for weeks. "You may want to rethink having me clean this place, Sir." He showed the cup to Nash.

"Yes, well…." He took the mug from Joshua, took it to the sink, and ran water into it. "I tend to lose track of time and obviously cleanliness while I'm out here."

"You're very good," Joshua commented as he took in Nash's art. "I once thought about being an artist. Wanted to go to Paris, set up an easel, and sell my drawings to those who passed by. Only one problem."

"Which is?"

"I suck at drawing. Can't even draw a proper stick figure." He chuckled.

"Yes, well, that would have made it a little difficult. Then again, I've seen some paintings that were priceless yet to me looked like someone threw paint at the canvas without any rhyme or reason."

"Kind of like that elephant who paints."

"Exactly! Art is in the eye of the beholder and some are apparently color blind or just simply blind."

Joshua couldn't help but laugh at the snort that escaped from Nash.

Curious, Joshua started to lift the cloth on a canvas that stood in the center of the room when Nash grabbed his wrist. "That one is a work in progress."

"Sorry."

"Don't be. I guess even out here, part of my irritating perfectionist side is still hanging out. How about we head back to the house and we can talk contract?"

"Okay."

Joshua glanced back at the covered painting before he stepped out the door. There were other works in progress that Nash hadn't covered, so he doubted Nash was being 100 percent honest about the perfectionist comment. Joshua's interest was certainly piqued as to why that particular painting was covered, but he didn't ask any further questions. He chalked it up to another thing he didn't understand about the man, but perhaps one day it would become clear. Or not. For now, he had a place to live for the next six months as long as he didn't fuck it up. For that, he was grateful and more than ready to sign the contract, regardless of the details written in it.

Back in the house, Nash led Joshua to his office. Nash took the seat behind the desk and pulled a file from a drawer. He took out a piece of paper from within it and handed it to Joshua. "It's pretty standard. You agree to give me your submission for six months. If it works out, we can sign a continuance as-is for another six, renegotiate certain terms or the time period, or end our association."

Joshua took the contract and scanned it, not really paying attention to the wording but looking for the place where his signature was required. "Do you have a pen?"

"I suggest you read it thoroughly before you sign. I do not want you using the excuse that you were unaware of the terms." Nash stood. "I'll give you a few minutes to read it over."

Without looking back, he left the office, closing the door behind him. Joshua took the chair on the opposite side of Nash's desk. He did as he was told, reading each line. This wasn't his first time with contracts, but once again, Nash surprised him. Most of it was pretty straightforward and similar to other documents he'd signed in the past. He was giving up his right to make personal decisions for himself and would be required to follow Nash's rules or be subjected to punishment. One line, however, was unlike anything he'd seen before.

For his gift of submission, I will see to it that Joshua's needs are met and that he never regrets giving such a gift.

Joshua read the line over and over, making sure he read it right and wasn't misinterpreting it. If he had any apprehensions over signing a contract with Nash—which he didn't—that one statement would have removed any doubt. He grabbed a pen from the holder and scribbled his signature and the date next to it.

He sat back in his chair, ran his hand over the stubble on his head, and propped his feet up on the desk. He stared at the ceiling, the line from the contract still playing in his head. Nash had mentioned something about their relationship being a journey. Joshua might not understand the man, still thought he was fricking weird, but he liked the way Nash talked. He especially liked the way he looked, his smile, his scent, pretty much everything about him. That didn't mean Joshua would let his guard down completely. Doms always had ulterior motives, but he'd stay, play the game, and hopefully it would work out and Nash would keep him around for a while.

He waited a few more minutes before grabbing the signed contract and heading out of the office. It was no surprise when he found Nash in the kitchen with yet another cup of coffee. Joshua leaned against the doorframe and smiled. "Too much caffeine can't be good for you."

Nash looked up and returned the smile. "I drink it from morning till night, and I will have you know I am exceptionally healthy."

"That's good to know." He set the contract down next to Nash. "That means you'll be around to fulfill this for the next six months."

Nash arched a brow. "Did you read all of it?"

"Yes, and I especially like that part where it says *for his gift of submission, I will see to it that Joshua's needs are met and that he never regrets giving such a gift.*"

"I meant every word, although I believe it's a pretty standard contract."

Joshua shook his head vigorously. "No, Sir, it's not. I mean, sure, some of it is. The stuff about rules, discipline, punishment, etc. Those things I've seen in a contract before, but how you describe my submission as a gift. That is…." He shook his head again. "It's why I didn't hesitate in signing it."

Nash met his gaze with a sincere expression. "I promise to care for you always." He pulled a pen out of a drawer and added his signature and date on the line beneath Joshua's. Then he folded it and put it and the pen back into the drawer before looking up at Joshua and smiling. "I think this calls for a little celebration, don't you?"

"Yes, Sir. How would you like to celebrate our union?"

Nash stepped up close to him and slid his arm around Joshua's waist, pulling him close. "How about we start with a kiss. You know, to seal the deal?"

Oh yeah, Nash was unlike any Dom Joshua had ever met. He reminded himself that if it was too good to be true, it probably was. Still, he moaned at the first press of Nash's lips against his, the sound increasing as the kiss deepened. Nash dominated the kiss and Joshua opened his mouth, going pliant and allowing Nash to explore and take what he needed. Joshua's body heated with the soft slide of tongue and Nash's flavor filling his mouth. His cock began to harden, and he pushed up against Nash, seeking out his warmth and a little friction. It had been days since he'd gotten off, and he suddenly found himself achingly hard. He rutted even more vigorously against Nash.

Although Nash's erection pressed against Joshua's, he obviously wasn't as needy as Joshua was as he ended the kiss and, to Joshua's great disappointment and frustration, stepped back.

"Normally we'd do coffee and then discipline before starting our day. But being that I feel it's a very important part of the day, we won't forgo it today even though it is later. Go stand in the center of the living room and strip."

Joshua's cock throbbed, and a thrill of anticipation raced down his spine. "Yes, Sir." He hurried to take his position, pulling his shirt off as he went. He folded his shirt and set it on the chair and then removed his sweatpants, giving them the same care before going to his display position.

Nash took a seat on the couch directly in front of Joshua. The look of appreciation on his face as he raked his eyes up and down Joshua's body thrilled Joshua. However, it was the heavy paddle covered in black leather and silver studs in Nash's hand that had Joshua thrumming.

"What is the purpose of discipline?" Nash asked.

"To remind me who is in charge." It was the same response Joshua had given each morning to Troy. Which, with the way Troy stood over him with a stern face and arms crossed over his chest while Joshua cleaned or cooked, it wasn't as if he would forget.

"If I am your Dom and you have signed a contract stating you accept the rules and the arrangement, why would you need daily reminders of my authority?"

My thoughts exactly. Joshua didn't say it out loud, but he was unsure of how to answer. "To remind your ego who is in charge" probably wasn't the right thing to say so he settled on vague. "I wouldn't, Sir. I know who is in charge but perhaps it's more of a reinforcement of that charge rather than a reminder."

Nash twirled the paddle in his hand. "I don't believe either of those is true. I have learned that with regular discipline, the need for punishment is often less."

Joshua was riveted by the swirl and sway of the paddle, his arousal growing with each beat of his heart, causing him to have a difficult time concentrating on words. All he wanted was that sting, to hear the thud, feel the heat, and fuck, he wanted to soar on the wings of pain. It had been too long, far too long since he'd reached a good high. Without taking his eyes from the paddle, Joshua nodded. "Yes, Sir."

"I believe I have lost your focus," Nash pointed out. "Perhaps you'll be more apt to listen to me during your spanking?"

"Yes, Sir."

IT WAS apparent what his boy wanted by the way Joshua's gaze never left the paddle and the way his body was visibly shaking. If that wasn't enough to clue Nash in, then the way Joshua's cock was straining and the light sheen of perspiration covering his body sure as hell was. Nash wouldn't get anywhere with Joshua until he was given what he wanted. But this wasn't only about Joshua, Nash needed this too.

He patted his lap. "Over my knees, boy."

Joshua's body flushed a lovely shade of pink as he bent, placing his hands on the floor on the opposite side of Nash's legs, his knees slightly bent to put himself in the perfect position to display his ass.

Nash set the paddle down and grabbed Joshua's ass, squeezing hard. "How long has it been since you've been paddled?"

"Far too long, Sir," Joshua moaned and shifted slightly, pressing his cock against the side of Nash's thigh, seeking friction.

Nash let Joshua rut as he continued to knead the firm muscles of Joshua's ass. With his free hand, he touched and encouraged Joshua to move until he was resting on his elbows and his ass was right there.

"You'll take ten swats, and you are to count them. You are not to come."

"Yes, Sir. Ten swats and I am not to come," Joshua replied as he settled further into position, still swaying slightly.

Nash picked up the paddle and, without warning, laid a hard swat on Joshua's ass.

Joshua cried out, jerking at the unexpected blow.

"Count them," Nash demanded and landed another blow.

"Oh! Oh! Damn, that felt good. Two. That's two, Sir."

The paddle came down again, the slap against bare skin loud and satisfying.

"Three." Joshua groaned.

"Good boy," Nash praised and used his free hand to rub Joshua's reddening ass, enjoying the heat against his palm. He then rewarded Joshua with another hit, a bit harder this time.

"F-four, Sir. Thank y—" His words momentarily cut off when Nash landed yet another swat that caused him to jerk, back arching a little. "Thank you, Sir. Five."

Nash slid his hand up to the center of Joshua's back, pushing him down, restricting his movements, and landed two more quick, hard blows.

"Ah, fuck!" Joshua cried out, but even as he did, he pushed his ass upward, begging for more with his body. "Six, seven."

"Discipline is about focus. It's not to remind you of who is in charge but to give you focus. I want you to feel me even when I'm not touching you," Nash purred and brought down the paddle again.

"Eight. Oh god, Sir. Thank you. Need to focus. Need to feel you."

"I will help you find your focus," Nash assured him and landed another blow, hitting the tops of Joshua's thighs.

Joshua tipped his head back, body going tense as he processed the blow. He didn't cry out, but blew out a long heavy breath and whispered, "Nine," before relaxing once again.

Nash took a moment to rub his palm over Joshua's heated flesh and enjoy his growing arousal. His cock was hard, and his excitement grew from the sight of his red marks on Joshua's ass. His marks. The marks he couldn't wait to push his groin against and feel the burning flesh as he fucked his boy.

"Last one," he warned and landed the final blow, the hardest one yet.

"Ow! Fuck yes!" Joshua jerked, but rather than pull away, he pushed his ass up. "Ten. Another? Please, one more."

Nash briefly considered giving him one more as he requested, but pushed the notion aside quickly. It would do neither of them any good at this point to give in so easily. Nash set the paddle aside and gave Joshua a little shove. "Hands and knees, boy."

Joshua whimpered his disappointment but did as Nash instructed. Nash slid from the couch and retrieved a condom and lube from the side table drawer. He was glad he'd thought ahead and made sure supplies were handy throughout the house. He took his time removing his pants and rolling the condom onto his hard dick while enjoying the sight of his boy's reddened ass. He slicked up his fingers and tossed the lube on the couch next to Joshua, then went to his knees behind him.

"This is quite stunning." Nash gave a quick tap to Joshua's ass.

"Feels good too." Joshua groaned, pushing his ass back. "I'm so hard, I ache, Sir."

Nash ran the slick down the crease of Joshua's ass. "I know what you want." He pressed his finger against Joshua's entrance, teasing just a bit. "And I'll always give you what you need," he promised before breaching Joshua's ass just a little. Joshua was tight, the small ring of muscles clamping down on his finger.

"More, Sir. Please." His boy was swaying, trying to take more of Nash's finger into him.

Nash grabbed a handful of Joshua's abused flesh, squeezing hard. "Be still, boy."

Again Joshua whimpered his disappointment, but did as he was told. His muscles shook, showing his restraint as he tried not to give in to what his body demanded.

Only when Joshua began to relax and he hung his head did Nash push his finger deeper into that tight hole. He pumped it in and out a few times until he pulled a satisfying sound from Joshua. "First I am going to take what I need." He slid a second finger in along the first. Joshua tensed with the invasion, but only for a single breath. "You can talk, beg, or scream, but you are not to come until I tell you. Is that understood?"

"Yes, yes, Sir. But please, please hurry and fuck me. Want it so bad."

Nash slapped Joshua's ass again hard, causing him to jerk. "Stop focusing on yourself. It will only end in disappointment. This is about my needs, my pleasure."

"I...." Joshua swallowed hard and let out another heavy breath. "Focus," he echoed, the statement no doubt more for his own need than for Nash's.

Nash could hear the desperation in Joshua's voice. Hell, Nash had been experiencing the same thing since the first time he'd touched Joshua, but he wasn't going to be rushed. He was going to savor every second of his first time entering his boy. *My boy.* Fuck, he loved the way that sounded and would never tire of saying it.

Nash slid his fingers from Joshua and wrapped them around his own prick, guiding it until it pressed against Joshua's slick hole. He then grabbed Joshua's ass in both hands, squeezing and kneading the taut, hot flesh.

Joshua groaned, muttering softly under his breath, the words indiscernible but not important, since he was about to make Joshua fly.

Nash leaned forward and slid his tongue along Joshua's spine, pressing a kiss to the back of his neck. "Are you ready for me?" Nash murmured against the soft skin.

"God, yes," Joshua moaned. "Fuck me, Sir."

Nash rubbed the head of his prick along Joshua's crack and then nudged again at his hole. He pushed in only far enough to breach Joshua, then backed off. Did it again. Gritting his teeth, he held back on what he wanted most: to shove himself deep in Joshua's tight heat.

Joshua began to pick up the rhythm Nash set, moving against him, rocking, pushing against his cock. The slow progress was maddening. Nash's breath came in short pants, pulse racing, his need to thrust nearly overwhelming him. He pushed in a little deeper. Joshua's tight ass clamped down on his cock, shredding Nash's restraint. He moved a little faster, pushed in a little deeper.

"God. your ass feels good," he groaned.

"So does your cock. Love the stretch, the burn."

"Going to fill you up so full, boy."

"Yes, Sir, please. Do it. More."

Nash couldn't deny them any longer. He splayed his hands on Joshua's ass and pushed in deeper, hips working to move in a little more on each thrust. It wasn't long before he was buried to the hilt, the heat of Joshua's reddened ass burning him.

Joshua gasped and tipped his head back, his body going tense for a few heartbeats. Nash's cock wasn't that long, but it was thick at the base and he knew it would take Joshua a few strokes to adjust to the burn. He held still, breathing harshly through his nose until Joshua dropped his head and blew out a breath.

Nash pulled all the way out and plunged in again causing Joshua to cry out. "Oh god." Joshua wriggled his ass, pushed back.

They rocked together, Joshua taking each hard thrust eagerly. Nash dug his fingers into the meaty flesh of Joshua's ass, using his boy as leverage as he fucked him hard and fast. Nash couldn't slow down if he wanted to. He'd have to work on his stamina, but not today. Joshua felt too good and Nash had been denied far too long. He shifted slightly, aiming for Joshua's gland as he pushed in.

Joshua threw his head back. "Fuck! Right there. Oh fuck, right fucking there," he babbled in between grunts and groans as Nash nailed his sweet spot over and over again.

So absorbed in the pleasure-filled sounds pouring from his boy and working his damnedest to keep them going, Nash was blindsided by his orgasm and defenseless to stop it. At the last second, he reached down and wrapped his fist around Joshua's cock. "Come with me," he demanded and jerked his boy off.

Joshua's body went still, muscles going incredibly tense, seconds before come poured over Nash's fist as he continued to slam into Joshua's ass, filling the condom in long pulses. After the last drop seeped from his body, he collapsed on Joshua's back, letting him hold his weight for a moment while he caught his breath and made his shaking muscles finally respond to his commands.

Nash pressed a gentle kiss to Joshua's shoulder and then groaned when he sat back and slipped from his boy's body. "Now that's what I call a celebration." Nash popped Joshua on the butt. He went to his feet, smiling at how weak his legs were and how fucking good he felt. "C'mon, you can wash me before you clean up your mess."

"Yes, Sir."

His smile grew as he headed to the shower and heard Joshua groan behind him. He was sure he wasn't the only one who was a little unsteady on his feet.

Chapter Nine

NASH WOKE with a start in the silent darkness. He blinked his eyes several times until they adjusted. Something had woken him, but nothing in the room seemed to be out of place, and the only sound was the faint whir of the ceiling fan. He stretched, yawning hugely. Giving up on figuring out what had disturbed him, he rolled over and snuggled into the warmth of the mattress.

As he lay there, the fog of sleep burned off and his brain finally caught up. *Coffee.* The rich scent of it brewing was what had pulled him from slumber. His next thought settled on Joshua, and he smiled. Having someone serve him coffee in bed was way better than a programmable brewer. The only thing that could make this morning better would be if he'd woken with Joshua sleeping next to him. That would come in time.

Although Joshua had been polite, done everything asked of him, and seemed eager to please, Nash had the feeling that Joshua was simply going through the motions. The real Joshua hid behind the mask of the perfect little sub he was portraying. Nash had to bring Joshua back from the edge and secure him within a safe boundary, but before he could do that, the walls Joshua surrounded himself with would need to come down. It wouldn't be easy, no way to plow into it so that it would crumble. This wall would have to be taken down painfully slowly, one brick at a time.

Nash scrubbed his hand over his face. Malcolm was right; this was to be an epic challenge. Not only did he have to help Joshua find safe limits, but he also had no fucking clue who he'd find behind the façade of the well-trained submissive.

The door squeaked, and a low light streamed in. Nash turned his head to find Joshua creeping through the door with a tray in hand. He sat up and leaned against the headboard. "Good morning, boy."

"Good morning, Sir. I'm sorry if I woke you. I forgot to ask if I was to have your coffee next to your bed when you woke."

"You didn't wake me. You are right on time." Nash turned on the bedside lamp and patted his lap. "You can set it right here."

Joshua set the tray where Nash instructed, then went to his knees next to the bed, his eyes lowered respectfully.

The tray was covered with a linen napkin, part of a set Nash had received as a gift and too fancy to use every day. Besides a mug of hot coffee, there was also a small stainless steel carafe he assumed was filled with more coffee, a sugar bowl, creamer and a spoon. Nash couldn't help but smile at how proper it all was, Joshua no doubt going all out to impress. Eventually, he'd learn a to-go mug filled to the brim with black coffee would suffice.

"This is quite the setup," Nash complimented. He picked up his mug, took a tentative sip, and, finding it the right temperature as not to burn his tongue, took a larger drink.

"I hope I didn't forget anything."

"No, actually, it's over-the-top." Joshua's shoulders slumped, and Nash quickly added, "I very much appreciate the time and effort you put into it, but it isn't necessary. My large mug of black coffee is all I need to start my day. That and good company. How did you sleep?"

"The bed is very comfortable, Sir."

"That's not what I asked."

"Oh, umm… right. I slept good or, um, well, Sir. I was a little nervous that the alarm wouldn't go off, so I kept waking up. Once I learn to trust the clock, I'm sure I'll sleep through the night. Like I said, it's a very comfortable bed."

"Did you have your own room at Troy's?"

"No, I hadn't earned one yet."

Nash pursed his lips. "You were with him for at least a couple of months, were you not?"

"Yes, Sir."

"And in all that time you weren't able to earn your own room? Oh wait, is it that Troy shared his room?"

"Yes. I slept on a pallet next to his bed."

"What?" Nash didn't even try to keep the outrage out of his voice. Who in the hell had their submissive sleep on the floor for two fucking months?

Joshua tilted his head slightly, and Nash got a glimpse of his eyes before he quickly lowered them. "You sound surprised. Troy isn't the first Dom who has made me sleep on the floor next to his bed. At least he didn't chain me to the bed by my collar."

Nash didn't miss the amusement in Joshua's tone. *What the fuck is wrong with me?* The practice of a sub sleeping on the floor next to his master's bed wasn't that uncommon. Hell, he'd known one who preferred it. Whatever the strange connection he had to Joshua was scattering his goddamn brain because the thought of Joshua being chained to a bed or sleeping on the floor pissed him off. Which was completely illogical. Oh damn, he needed a sounding board.

Nash leaned over and petted Joshua's head. "I simply don't understand that practice. I'm a bit of a cuddle whore and like to wake up with a warm body wrapped around mine. One of your priorities is to earn that right. Is that understood?"

"Yes, Sir," Joshua responded, the amusement still in his tone.

"All right, then. You can take this tray to the kitchen and get breakfast started." He wrapped his hands around his mug. "You may not, however, have this."

"Anything in particular you want to eat, Sir?"

"Surprise me."

Nash waited until Joshua removed the tray and exited the room. Only then did he roll his eyes at himself. He finished his cup of much-needed caffeine, took care of his morning business, and stopped by his office before heading to the kitchen. Sitting at his desk, he dialed the familiar number.

The phone rang several times, and Nash was about to hang up when Malcolm's sleepy voice came through the line. "You better be dead or dying, calling me at this ungodly hour."

"Good morning, sunshine," Nash said in a chipper voice.

"Ugh! Good-bye."

"Don't you dare hang up on me. I need you."

There was a slight pause, and then Nash heard Malcolm groan. "Do you need me so early in the morning?"

Nash leaned back in his chair. "You're getting old, Malcolm. How many times in the past have you woken me at the ass crack of dawn?"

"This is not about me unless it's about me going back to sleep."

"Not a chance. I do believe it is your fault I have this early-rising habit."

Nash had always been more of a night owl until he'd met Malcolm. Back then, Malcolm was of the belief if he didn't rise till after eight, he'd wasted the day away. While Nash had been mentored by Malcolm, he'd gotten used to getting up early. After his contract with Malcolm expired, they had often chatted on the phone over their morning coffee since they'd remained such good friends.

"Yes, well, these subs nowadays have no concept of time, wanting to play until the sun comes up," Malcolm drawled. "Anyway, please tell me what I can do to help you so I can go back to sleep."

"I keep losing my focus with Joshua and I have no idea how to control my crazy thoughts. This morning I became outraged upon learning that, in the past, Joshua was chained and made to sleep on the floor. Joshua obviously thought I was fucking nuts—which apparently I am—because I swear I heard the laughter in his voice when he responded to my shock." Nash reached for his goatee and, finding it no longer there, gritted his teeth and dropped his hand. "I know plenty of Doms who practice that—hell, I even know a few subs who prefer it—so what is wrong with me? What is it about this boy that has me so messed up?"

"I don't know, seeing as I've never seen you react to another man like you do Joshua. Hmmm… perhaps this is a good argument for love at first sight."

Nash was glad Malcolm couldn't see the way he rolled his eyes. "I assure you I am not in love with Joshua."

"Then the only other possibility is that you feel sorry for him, which, for his situation and his needs, is even worse."

Dammit! Nash did feel sorry for Joshua. How could he not? His road map of scars outlined years of abuse and torture. He had no money, nowhere to live, and didn't even own anything besides the clothes on his back. "You're right."

"I usually am," Malcolm pointed out. "You'd better get that under control, and if you are unable to, my suggestion would be to look for someone who can take care of Joshua properly. Because Joshua doesn't need your pity, he needs your help."

"I know this."

"Then why are you calling me?"

"Just because I know it, doesn't mean I know how to control it. I want to do the right thing for Joshua, and I am *not* giving him up. So stop being grumpy and tell me what to do to get my focus back."

"You know what to do," Malcolm said curtly.

Nash growled.

"Ooh, I like it when you growl. It's sexy as fuck."

"Malcolm."

"What? You *are* sexy as fuck when you growl, and you are also a good Dom. You've simply lost sight of that with the strong emotional attraction you have for the boy. If he is willing to set aside everything for you and your pleasure, then the very least you can do is reward him for that. For the time being, stop focusing on Joshua's past and concentrate on his immediate needs. Keep it simple and take it one minute, one hour at a time. You'll have plenty of time later, once trust is established, to work on the bigger issues."

One minute at a time. It was easier said than done. Every time Nash got a glimpse of the sadness in Joshua's eyes or Joshua slumped in despair or disappointment, Nash's chest tightened a little. Each time he looked upon the scars, his heart hurt. As his shortcomings came to him, so did a plan, and even though he was no longer addressing his thoughts toward Malcolm, he said them aloud. "I need to stop focusing on Joshua's scars. It serves me no purpose at this time to dwell on the past, only the present. Joshua will need to keep his eyes respectfully low. I can't be a witness to his sadness or disappointment but need to focus on what he can do. One minute, one hour at a time."

"I couldn't have said it better myself," Malcolm praised. "Call me and let me know how it works out. After the sun comes up." The line went dead.

Nash set the phone back on its cradle. He pulled a pen and a pad of paper from the drawer of his desk and scribbled out a list of things to do, the first being: focus on what's best for Joshua and not himself.

KNEELING AT Nash's side, Joshua's tension increased with each tick of the clock. Nash hadn't said more than a few words during breakfast. Even with the frequent glances Joshua had stolen while they ate, he couldn't get a read on Nash. His Dom's expression was neutral, not giving off a single indication of what he was thinking or feeling.

Without warning, Nash went to his feet and waved a hand toward his empty plate. "Get this cleaned up and meet me in the safe room."

Joshua nodded. "Certainly, Sir."

"And Joshua?" Nash waited until Joshua met his gaze. There was a flash of desire in Nash's eyes, but seconds later it was gone, leaving Joshua to wonder if he'd actually seen it. Nash's tone cool when he added, "Do I have to remind you I don't like to be kept waiting?"

"No, Sir. I remember. I will be quick."

Joshua gathered up the dirty dishes, all the while feeling Nash's eyes on him. He didn't dare look back up, instead concentrating on getting busy with his chores. It wasn't until he was standing at the sink, his back to Nash, that he heard the man's footsteps fading as he moved down the hall.

Joshua stared into the sink as the water from the tap swirled the bubbles. He hoped it was desire he'd seen in Nash's gaze because Joshua's head was aching as were his balls. *Don't make me wait too long.* Regardless of what he'd agreed to, Joshua was tempted to make Nash fucking wait. Perhaps if he got the man riled up enough, pissed him off a little, Nash would actually put some weight behind his swings. Or maybe he should make up some excuse for why he needed to go out. Prowl the streets and back alleys and find someone who got off on dishing out true pain.

He needed to find a brutal man who cared little for another's suffering. He wanted to suffer. Wanted the bite of leather, torn skin, abuse to his flesh that would wash away the pain in his head. No Dom/sub rules, no restrictions. No societal pressure. No bullshit. Just pain and peace.

Joshua gripped the edges of the sink tightly, needing the support as his legs shook. He battled with two conflicting needs. Oh god, and how he needed to find some peace. Having spent the last two nights awake with nothing to focus on but his own thoughts, he needed relief. Needed to fucking soar and get lost in something besides his mind. Yet, to leave, to seek out easing of his physical and mental needs was to give up a place to sleep, clean clothes, food.

Fuck!

Chapter Ten

"ENTER."

Joshua pushed the door open, the battle of whether to stay or run still wreaking havoc on his body. Each step was laborious. Nash was leaning a shoulder against the wall, his arms crossed over his chest. Joshua was definitely attracted to him, but it was the intense dark gaze and the stern expression on his face that had Joshua going to the center of the room. He'd stay for now. He could always change his mind later.

"What are you looking for?"

Pain. Thankfully, Joshua had the good sense not to blurt it out even if it was true. Nash claimed he wanted complete honesty, but did he really? If Joshua gave Nash what he was asking for, could he handle it? Would he simply send Joshua and his fucked-up self away?

What are you looking for?

Joshua gritted his teeth. He hated that fucking question. He never knew how to answer it in a way that would satisfy the man asking it. They all were seeking a different answer. Joshua considered what he knew so far about Nash, choosing his words carefully. "I'm looking for a master. I'm looking for someone who can control me. I'm looking for you, Sir."

Nash's stern expression didn't change, but he gave a curt nod. "On your knees."

Joshua didn't hesitate. If he was going to stay, going to give Nash another chance, then he'd play his role perfectly. For now.

Nash pushed off the wall and came to stand before Joshua. He planted his feet slightly apart, hands on his hips. "Service me."

Something had changed in Nash after Joshua had left his bedroom earlier. This was a test. The snap in Nash's voice, his hard expression, and his demanding demeanor sent a thrill racing down Joshua's spine.

Maybe he'd read him wrong. Maybe he wasn't soft, weak.

THERE WAS no hesitation. Nash gave nothing away, determined in his new resolve, his veneer of control as his cock was freed from his pants. Joshua took the head of Nash's cock into his mouth, lips pulled back to protect Nash's flesh from teeth.

Nash moaned his approval, giving Joshua something for his easy acceptance of Nash's cock. Knowing this wasn't what Joshua was hoping for when he entered the room, Nash didn't care. Joshua would have to learn to accept Nash's will. Nash was in control at this moment. Nothing else mattered except his own pleasure and that Joshua bend to his will.

Nash pushed deeper, wanted to make him sweat, make him unbalanced and force him to focus on Nash, work for his approval. Nash took Joshua's head in his hands, held him so he couldn't move his face back. Nash didn't thrust, had no intentions of fucking Joshua's mouth hard. Cool. Calm. Controlled. Nash slowly pushed his cock all the way into Joshua's throat, hesitated for a moment, cutting off Joshua's breath, pushing him, then just as slowly pulled it back to where only the tip rested on Joshua's lips.

Joshua breathed heavily through his nose, the only indication the deep penetration of his throat had affected him. Other than that, he held perfectly still, allowing Nash to set the pace, to take what he wanted.

Nash rolled his hips, found a slow, steady rhythm, enjoying the sensation of his growing arousal at a pace that wouldn't take him to the edge too quickly. He liked having Joshua on his knees before him. The sight of the man, the warm wet mouth, the power Nash held over him was intoxicating.

Nash didn't praise, didn't say a word, concentrating on chasing his orgasm, one slow stroke at a time. He took the opportunity to reestablish his power over the man, to solidify his resolve and think about nothing but his own pleasure, his will, his need.

Joshua was a talented little cocksucker. While he remained still, didn't try to hamper Nash's movements, he used his teeth and tongue, demanding Nash's orgasm. Nash tried to hold back, held out as long as he could to deny that demand, but far too soon Nash was emptying into Joshua's throat.

Joshua didn't miss a drop. He swallowed, throat contracting around Nash's dick, prolonging Nash's pleasure until he was spent and limp.

Nash eased his grip on Joshua's head, and he slid his hand down to cup Joshua's jaw, cock slipping from his mouth. "Well done, boy. Now we'll see if you take my crop as easily as you take my dick."

Nash didn't miss the way Joshua shuddered or the excitement in his tone when he said, "Yes, Sir."

Nash made him wait. He knew this was the reward Joshua was hoping for, but Nash wasn't going to make it easy. He held Joshua's jaw and waited, staring into those expressive green eyes, not saying a word.

It took Joshua several long moments to calm himself. Obviously his focus was on his own needs rather than Nash's. Finally, after what seemed like an eternity, Joshua relinquished his control once again. He relaxed and leaned into Nash's touch.

"That's it," Nash murmured. "So beautiful when you submit. You will be even more so with my marks on your skin, dancing beneath my crop."

"Thank you, Sir."

"What are your safewords?" Nash asked, not sure Joshua would use them but needing to reiterate their importance to Joshua.

"Yellow and red, Sir."

Nash used to think that there was no point of living the lifestyle if boundaries weren't pushed. Now he wondered if he'd been thinking about it all wrong. Maybe right now it wasn't his job to push boundaries or even to set them. Perhaps his job was to concentrate on his needs being met as well as the needs of his boy. They could press limits—or find them—later, after they were more comfortable with each other.

"Get up. Leave your clothes here and follow me." Nash had to clamp down on his excitement. It had been a very long time since he'd used his playroom, and the thought of having Joshua there thrilled him.

Joshua followed to heel quietly, but the sharp intake of breath when they entered the playroom and the lights were turned on had

Nash fighting back his smile. He was very proud of this room, had spent years adding to his collection. He'd meticulously planned out every aspect of the room to suit his needs. The rubberized black walls and ceiling were designed for both easy cleanup and to add to the other soundproofing measure hidden behind the walls. Joshua could scream as loud as he wanted and it would never escape past the door.

Shackles hung from the ceiling by heavy chains; thick metal O-rings were bolted to the floor in various locations. A leather-bound St. Andrew's cross and a spanking bench, as well as an exam table, took up the space on one side. But it was the vast collection of crops, whips, paddles, and floggers that caught Joshua's attention when he went to the center of the room and stood in his display position. His long slender cock was hard and stretching up and away from his body and his head was tilted toward the implements, no doubt trying to see them without turning.

Without a word, Nash went to the armoire and threw open the doors. He studied the contents. He picked up a heavy metal anal plug and considered it for a moment. The weight of it would force Joshua to keep his focus on it while he was being cropped or it would slip from his body. Joshua needed that focus on something other than the pain, but the plug wasn't quite right. Nash set it back down. He wanted Joshua to need Nash's cock filling him while Nash beat him.

He grabbed a condom and a small tube of lube and slid them into the front pocket of his pants. He then chose a metal cock ring with a locking spring system. It was smooth and wouldn't dig into sensitive flesh, but it would cause a lot of pressure around Joshua's cock, much like a very tight fist.

"Stand beneath the chains," Nash ordered and pointed to the ones attached to shackles so there would be no confusion.

Joshua moved into position without argument.

Running his fingers over the cool surface of the cock ring, Nash watched him move, the lean muscles of Joshua's legs flexing with each step and his cock bobbing. Nash took a moment to appreciate Joshua's impressive body as well as to give himself a chance to clear his mind. He grounded himself in this moment, setting aside the past and the future. Only the here and now.

Joshua's gaze stayed on Nash's hands as the shackles were placed around Joshua's wrists. Nash slid a single finger beneath the steel. Satisfied the bindings weren't too tight, he adjusted the length of the chain so Joshua had to go up on his toes, body stretched. Nash then set his focus on Joshua's hard cock. He pumped it a couple of times before securing the cock ring. Joshua sucked in a harsh breath, body going rigid for a few heartbeats, vulnerable balls lifting as he adjusted to the pressure. Nash watched him carefully, ready to remove the ring if it became too much. But then Joshua closed his eyes and blew out a long breath, the tension leaving his body.

God, he's beautiful. Joshua was strong yet vulnerable, a heady mixture, and Nash's desire for him increased. He wanted him. All of him. Not just his body, but his mind, his heart, his very soul.

Focus, he reminded himself. *Here and now. Nothing else matters.*

"You are not to come unless I give you permission. Is that understood?"

"Yes, Sir. I won't, Sir," Joshua responded, his voice tight.

Nash went to the wall, which was covered by his collection of implements. Although his back was to Joshua, he could feel his gaze boring into him. Or maybe it was the way Nash brushed his fingers over the soft wood of the cane that intrigued Joshua. Didn't matter. Let him watch. Nash picked up various items, all for show. Let Joshua wonder and let his excitement grow. Finally, Nash picked up the riding crop with the ring of black leather attached to the end.

Nash turned around and tested the crop against his thigh. The snap caused Joshua's eyes to flash for a second, a single heartbeat, and then he lowered his eyes and licked his lips.

Evidence of Joshua's excitement was written all over his body, the way he swayed, the slight increase in the rise and fall of his chest, and the light sheen of perspiration glistening on his brow. Joshua was so fucking beautiful it hurt. And he would hurt too.

Nash had no silly notions that he would break Joshua with a single cropping. But there was a part of him that still clung to the hope that the others were wrong. That Joshua wasn't as far gone as Kirk claimed he was. Nash was a realist, though. There would be no disappointment if the boy didn't break; it would only further cement

Nash's conviction that eventually he would. Joshua needed to know that he couldn't manipulate Nash. That if Joshua put his trust in him, he could push him over that edge, allow him to soar and be there to catch him. Nash would not fail him as others had.

The tension in the room built to a palpable thing that took on a life of its own. It swirled around them, cocooning them with their expectations, excitement, hope. It caused the air to become heavy, a bitter scent of need infusing it.

"You're to stay still and not make a sound until you can no longer hold it back. Is that understood?" Nash needed to know, needed a mark of Joshua's tolerance.

"I understand, Sir."

"Good. We begin." Nash came to stand behind Joshua and drew his arm back. In the second before he let his arm fall, Nash had the distinct feeling that the events about to take place were of the utmost importance. Possibly the most important thing he'd ever done. He could not fail Joshua. *I won't.* He let the crop fly.

The skin on Joshua's left shoulder went white and then, a heartbeat later, turned a lovely shade of red. Nash's strike was placed with the perfect amount of weight, the mark undeniable.

He laid another one down on the opposite shoulder.

It took six or seven strokes before Joshua showed any outward sign of feeling the blows. But then there was a low, barely audible rumbling sound and it was like music to Nash's ears.

Joshua was strong. Nash had never met anyone who could take that many blows without so much as a grunt. But it thrilled Nash that Joshua did, in fact, have limits. Seven blows before he made a sound was a limit, a small one, but still a limit nonetheless. If he could find one that easily, then he was sure he'd find others. Kirk was an idiot. *Focus.*

Nash's next strokes were laid against the juncture of thigh and ass. Joshua's head was tipped back and turned just enough that Nash was able to see his eyes flutter closed, but that was the only response to the strikes.

Nash adjusted his swing, but not the weight behind it, letting the next one land across Joshua's ass. Nash smiled when the muscles of Joshua's backside tightened and he went up even farther on his toes for a split second. He'd felt it and couldn't not respond to it, no matter how subtle. Nash saw it and took joy in the fact that Joshua wasn't made of stone. That he wouldn't just stand there with no response and allow Nash to beat him to death. Nash only had to watch for the small responses, keep a critical eye on Joshua's flesh as not to do any permanent damage, and back off at just the right moment that would give Joshua the pleasure he sought in pain while not letting him fall into the abyss.

Nash took his focus off Joshua for a moment while he processed everything, so the period before the next stroke landed was longer. Again only the smallest of response, a small gasp, but Nash would take it. It became a battle between them. A fight to see who actually had control. Would Nash's arm give out before Joshua gave him something more? Would his strength strip Nash of his control?

No. Nash refused to give up even the tiniest amount. This was his realm, his show, his outcome to decide. Nash knew even with holding back on the power of his strikes, that enough strikes could cause Joshua's skin to tear. He refused to spill a single drop of Joshua's blood, at least not tonight. Perhaps one day, but only when Nash was 100 percent certain that he could read Joshua's body and know that he wasn't going to take it too far.

It took nearly twenty blows before Nash was rewarded with his first true response. The leather tip connecting with Joshua's balls caused him to cry out and his head fell forward. His breathing sped, he was panting, and a barely audible word was whispered. Nash didn't know what the boy had said, but it was enough that he'd let out a sound. Nash smiled again.

Another limit.

That deserved a reward. Nash lowered his arm and moved up close. He dragged his tongue along the base of Joshua's neck, tasting the salty sweat on his skin. A soft, needy sound escaped Joshua that caused a fine crack in Nash's control. Had anyone ever showed this man kindness or had they only taken, taken, and taken? Nash's gut roiled, the urge to wrap his arms around the man and hold him overwhelming, but he pushed it down.

Focus.

Nash brushed his lips along Joshua's shoulder, then stepped back. He raised his arm, let the crop fly again, let it kiss the spot where his lips were seconds ago. The dam broke. Joshua was no longer able to hold still and low sounds poured from his throat.

Nash's pulse raced, entire body tingling from arousal and pride. His arm was heavy with the effort of wielding the crop. His concentration narrowed down to nothing but Joshua and landing the stripes where he wanted them, where they would produce the greatest effect.

Another strike, another lovely cry. They worked together like perfectly synced music, the slaps complementing the pleasure-filled song. The skin of Joshua's back was a fiery red color, welts standing out above the white scars. Any more and his flesh would break. Nash refused to lay another strike to the swollen and bruised flesh. He moved around to stand in front of Joshua.

Nash's breath hitched at the sight before him. Joshua's face was slack in pleasure, his eyes glazed. Tracks of tears glistened on his cheeks, cock still hard. He was fully immersed in his subspace. He was flying and beyond beautiful.

Nash shortened the grip on the crop, giving him more control, then flicked the leather flap against Joshua's right nipple.

Joshua's eyes fluttered closed again, and his head fell back. The strike to his nipple caused the nub to tighten immediately, and Joshua's sharp cry echoed around the room.

Nash hit the other nipple, getting another lovely cry for his effort.

Knowing that in this moment, there would be no trace of sadness, only pleasure, Nash said, "Open your eyes."

Joshua gasped, his body bowstring tight, scarcely breathing, and shook his head.

"I said open your eyes," Nash demanded, tone hard and sharp like the crop, which he let fly again, hitting Joshua's pec slightly above his right nipple.

"Oh fuck!" Joshua cried out, glassy green eyes flying open.

Nash held his gaze for a moment, but he wasn't sure Joshua was really seeing him. No matter, he'd followed Nash's command, had stayed focused on his Dom while absorbing, processing the pain. Without looking away from those beautiful eyes, Nash leaned forward and slowly teased one of the abused nubs with the tip of his tongue, easing the sting and burn with soft, delicate flicks.

Joshua's eyes cleared and filled with pure need. Nash was overjoyed at the progress of their play. Joshua didn't fight him, didn't demand more; he took what Nash dished out, took it into himself and turned it into bright and shining pleasure. It was really quite breathtaking to witness.

As Nash continued to move his mouth back and forth across Joshua's chest, the man began to vibrate, as if he were having a harder time dealing with the soft touches than he had with the stinging slaps of the crop.

Joshua's lips parted as he panted. His hard cock was mere inches from Nash's mouth. The temptation was too much and he bent farther still to tease his tongue over the flared head. He reached out with his free hand, grabbed Joshua's balls, tugging, twisting them, not enough to cause real pain but to mimic the heavy pressure the cock ring produced.

Joshua stretched, tried to pull away, but his bindings kept him right there. He was at Nash's mercy. "There is nowhere to go," Nash murmured. Another flick of the tongue, a heavier tug to those delicate balls before Nash stood up and took a step back.

"Nowhere I'd rather be, Sir." Joshua pulled at his chains, making them rattle, adding to their shared music.

Joshua was on the edge; Nash could practically see him teetering on it. A few more strikes, a couple of hard pulls on his pulsing cock, and the boy, *his* boy would be coming. They stood there in that perfect moment, eyes locked. It was Nash's choice; his will determined which direction they would take or even if he'd allow Joshua to come. The power over such an amazing creature was heady, and he wavered on what he wanted to do next.

After a long, drawn-out moment, Nash raised the crop and placed a short stroke across Joshua's belly and then quickly followed it with another one, crossing the first one.

"Ah, god." Joshua arched for a second and then dropped his head, pressed his chin to his chest, panting harshly, his long hair covering his face. But Nash didn't need to see it to know the strikes had caused Joshua immense pleasure. The wild twitching of his cock, the flush of skin, were all the proof Nash needed.

Nash allowed the crop to fall from his fingers and crash to the floor. He placed his palm close to Joshua's stomach, not quite touching, and felt the heat. He pulled his shirt over his head and tossed it to the side. He moved to stand behind Joshua, the same ghost of a touch, the amount of heat radiating off Joshua amazing, satisfying. Nash slid his hands around Joshua's body, pressed them against the marks on Joshua's belly and tugged until his back was pressed to Nash's chest.

Joshua hissed. Nash could tell he wanted to pull away from the initial contact, but he didn't. He submitted, relaxing once again and allowing Nash to hold him.

"You are so amazing," Nash whispered against Joshua's ear. "I've never met anyone who could take a strike with as much composure as you do. How long you held in your sounds, kept your body still, was quite remarkable." He slid his lips down, tasting the salt of Joshua's skin, nipped at the tender flesh at the juncture of neck and shoulder. "So proud of you, boy."

Joshua moaned at the stinging bite, then turned his head, lips parted as if begging a kiss.

Nash didn't deny him. He pressed their mouths together, kissed him until they were both breathless. Nash's arms trembled from the tight hold, his muscles exhausted, but he couldn't rest, not yet. He reached up and detached Joshua's wrists from the shackles, catching him when he slumped.

Joshua tried to steady himself, to find his feet and stand, but Nash wasn't the only one exhausted because he allowed Nash to hold his weight awhile longer.

"I have you," Nash assured him. "Just rest for a minute, breathe."

When the trembling in Joshua's legs began to quiet, Nash led him out of the room, keeping him close as they made it into the safe room. Nash helped him to sit on the leather ottoman and then went to the cabinet and retrieved the first aid kit.

"Arms at your sides," Nash instructed him and then sprayed Joshua's wounds with anesthetic. The medicine was cool on Joshua's reddened flesh, and he tensed, goose bumps blooming across his skin. Nash inspected each and every strike, making sure the skin wasn't split. He found no evidence of a seeping wound but they were an angry red, and some had already begun to bruise. Satisfied with his marks, Nash returned the kit to the cabinet, then helped Joshua to the bed.

Lying on his side, Joshua did not let his gaze leave Nash's. So many emotions shone in his expressive eyes: pleasure, contentment, want, need, question. Nash wasn't sure which was more prominent. "How do you feel?"

"My body is ready for rest but… my mind…. I need something more," he admitted, voice hoarse.

"I know what you need. What *we* need." Nash took the condom and lube from his pocket before sliding out of his pants. He then joined Joshua on the bed, moving up behind him. Nash rolled on the condom and slicked it up before tossing the tube to the floor. He grabbed Joshua's leg and pushed it up and over to allow Nash to work his way slowly, oh so fucking slowly, into Joshua's ass.

Joshua moaned low, seductively when Nash breached him, the sounds growing in strength the deeper Nash pushed, Joshua's body taking him in with only the slightest hesitation. His ass was tight, gripping Nash's cock like a glove, squeezing it.

"Sir…." The single word was like a prayer passing Joshua's parted lips.

"I'm right here. Going to give you what you need."

Nash set a slow and steady pace and reached around to take Joshua's hard cock in hand, stroking it in time with the movements of his hips, finding that familiar rhythm they'd achieved during the beating. Their bodies danced perfectly against each other.

There was no rush. It was slow, almost sweet, lovemaking that pushed Nash higher and higher. How long they rocked together, Nash had no clue. He didn't care, wanting to stay in the moment, enjoy the experience. But it couldn't last forever. Nash pressed a kiss to Joshua's ear and whispered, "Come for me." He released the ring from Joshua's cock. One more thrust and he tumbled over the edge, not with a shout, but with a contented sigh. Joshua quickly followed, as if he'd needed Nash's release before he could achieve his own.

Nash rested his head on the pillow next to Joshua's, holding him tight, still buried deep within him, unwilling to release him. He placed a soft kiss on the back of Joshua's head, breathing him in.

It was in that moment, in the warm afterglow of their bliss that Nash realized that not only did Joshua belong to him, but he belonged to Joshua. He couldn't imagine ever touching another man this way. Didn't want to. A connection so strong bound him to Joshua in a way Nash had never experienced. He'd work hard, be the best he could be, so Joshua wouldn't ever want another's touch.

Chapter Eleven

AN UNSEASONABLE cold snap had blown through Michigan the day before. While the calendar confirmed it was midsummer, the weather suggested otherwise. Nash held out a jacket for Joshua to shrug into and then grabbed another one from the closet for himself. July and he was wearing a coat.

Fucking Michigan weather.

They stepped out the front door and Nash shivered as the cold wind hit his exposed neck and skittered down his spine. He zipped up his coat before shoving his hands into the deep pockets. "Jesus, I've heard of Christmas in July, but not winter," he teased. "You would have to pick today to want to explore the property."

Joshua tipped his head back and looked up at the dark overcast sky. "I love this weather. I'm not a huge fan of summer, or winter for that matter. I'd be perfectly happy with this temperature all year-round."

"Don't you dare wish away my nice weather," Nash chastised lightly. "I could compromise on say… seventies year-round but the fifties and sixties, nope. A little too chilly for me."

"Seventies, huh?" Joshua asked with a skeptical expression. Then he grinned and nodded. "Deal."

They walked shoulder to shoulder past the workshop and down the lane that led to the woods beyond. Neither of them said anything. Nash was deep in thought, playing over and over in his head what had occurred the night before. To others, it might not have been the same success it was to Nash, but learning he could easily read the small changes in Joshua and discovering how much pain to inflict before he got a reaction was huge. For the first time since meeting Joshua, Nash thought he might actually be able to handle the man's issues. He was happy over the events and also stunned at the way their lovemaking had gone. And that's what it was in the end. Not fucking, not simply getting a nut, but something more, a true connection forged. Or maybe it was simply an evolution of that spark Joshua had ignited in him the first time Nash had spotted him. Nash kept glancing at Joshua, wondering if he was also evaluating the evening before. But Joshua didn't appear to be thinking much beyond what he was seeing, taking in everything around him with a childlike wonder.

Stepping into the tree line and onto the well-worn footpath, Joshua whistled. "Wow, this is beautiful." He inhaled deeply. "And it smells good too."

Nash was extremely proud of his land. The first time he'd set foot in the house, he hadn't been impressed. It had been dated, and the fact that every wall had been covered with a horrible floral wallpaper and an equally ugly matching border nearly had him running from the place. It was the large workshop and land that had him signing on the dotted line. Being able to enjoy the outdoors and the seclusion the property afforded him made all those hours of scraping off the wallpaper worth it. Still, he'd never really thought about how the land smelled. It amazed him how in tune Joshua was with his surroundings.

Nash took a deep breath in through his nose. Now that Joshua had pointed it out, Nash became aware of the ignored sense. There was a hint of the wildflowers that dotted the landscape as well the musky aroma of earth and decaying vegetation. Joshua was right, it really did smell wonderful.

"You never cease to amaze me."

"Me?" Joshua sounded a bit confused. "What did I do, Sir?"

"Just being you."

Joshua wrinkled his nose in apparent disapproval and shook his head. "Then it wasn't the good kind of amazement."

"I beg to differ."

Joshua didn't say anything in response, simply shrugged.

Obviously, it wasn't only Joshua's addiction to pain Nash needed to address. Joshua's self-worth would need quite a bit of work too.

"If you could change one thing about yourself, what would it be?" Nash asked.

"That I wasn't dumb," Joshua responded without hesitation. The speed in which he came up with the answer was telling.

"You are far from dumb. The way in which you took over the kitchen, the amazing meals and flavors you can put together show that. You also speak well, follow directions and think things through. If you were dumb, you wouldn't be able to do that."

"Street smarts and my ability to manipulate people for my own gain isn't the same thing," Joshua pointed out.

Nash was struck by just how negatively Joshua viewed himself. The root of it was deep-seated and, he suspected, had been cultivated by the numerous people in his life who mistreated him. It hadn't taken Nash long to realize how special and wonderful Joshua was, but that wasn't enough. Joshua had not only to say it but believe it. Arguing with the man over it wasn't going to do that.

"Are you manipulating me?"

Joshua tilted his head up and looked at Nash from beneath his long lashes. "Of course I am," he said curtly.

"Oh really?"

"Of course. Isn't that what you do with me? Manipulate the situation to get what you want from me?"

Nash's brows dipped. "Hmm, I don't think I like that word. I prefer to call it...." Nash thought about it for a moment and really couldn't come up with a better definition. Still, *manipulate* had a negative connotation and the last thing they needed was more negativity when it came to Joshua's way of thinking. "We'll come up with a new name to describe our interactions."

"Like?"

"I don't know. I'll get back to you on that. But no more negative words, got it?"

"Yes, Sir." Joshua smirked.

They walked through the canopy of trees, the cool temperatures even more intense in the shade, and Nash was glad he'd chosen a warm fleece-lined jacket.

A thought suddenly occurred to Nash. "Joshua, did you finish high school?"

"Yeah, just barely, but I squeaked by."

Good. Nash could work with that. "What was your favorite subject?"

Joshua lifted a sagging branch that was blocking the way, allowing them to move deeper into the woods before he responded. "My favorite was history. Art would have been a close second. I sucked in both, but I liked them."

There was that negativity again. "You're more than welcome to use any of the supplies in the workshop if you'd like to create a little art of your own."

Joshua shook his head. "Thank you, but I'd just mess it up. Besides, like I said, I can't even draw a stick figure, but the history of art fascinates me."

"Ah, so it's the masters of the past that fascinate you. Who are some of your favorites?"

"I read a book called *Michelangelo and the Pope's Ceiling*—"

"Seriously?" Nash asked incredulously. It was a book only true lovers of Renaissance art and Michelangelo would have read. "I loved that book. I would never have guessed you'd read that."

"I do know how to read," Joshua grumbled.

Nash laid his hand against the small of Joshua's back. "I didn't mean it that way. It's not a typical book someone would read for pleasure. Usually, it's one pushed on an art student who complains about it."

"Someone had left it on the table at the library. I thought it sounded interesting, so I read it." Joshua shrugged. "I liked it."

Nash smiled at him and pulled him close to his side. He placed a kiss on Joshua's temple. "I liked it too."

Toward the back of the property, they found a large oak tree that had fallen close to the stream. Nash took a seat on it and tilted his head up toward the sun that had peeked out from behind the clouds, enjoying the way it warmed his chilled cheeks.

Joshua strolled along the stream, tossing in stones and watching them skip along the rippling water. Each time he turned his head toward Nash, Nash could see the look of concentration on his face. After the intensity of the night before, Nash didn't want to push, figuring Joshua needed time to process his new environment, but Nash was dying to know what he was thinking about.

Nash held back from asking as long as he could, but it was driving him fucking nuts. "I see steam coming from your ears. Care to share what's got your mind smoking?"

"I wasn't really thinking about anything," Joshua said, his back to Nash as he continued to toss rocks into the water.

"We're always thinking about something," Nash pointed out.

Joshua looked at Nash over his shoulder and hesitated. "Guess I should have said I wasn't thinking about anything important."

The lie was written on Joshua's features and in the way he had hesitated before he answered. Nash patted the log, gesturing Joshua over. "C'mere and have a seat."

Joshua dropped the rock in his hand and did as Nash asked. Once Joshua sat, Nash slid his arms around Joshua's waist, feeling the tension in the muscles. "How about I share what I was thinking about?"

"Sure." The fact that Joshua didn't address Nash as Sir and the curt way he spoke were sure signs something was weighing heavily on his mind.

Nash didn't call him out on it, not wanting to cause any more tension in Joshua, wanting his honesty.

"I was actually wondering about you. You've shared your likes and dislikes when it comes to the lifestyle, but what about in general?"

Joshua shrugged again.

Nash swallowed down his sigh. This was going to be like pulling teeth. Novocaine, aka easy questions, first. "What's your favorite food?"

"Italian."

"Great! That's one of mine too. Favorite sport?"

"I don't watch sports."

"Not even motocross or extreme sports? I figured you'd enjoy them considering you admitted to being an adrenaline junkie and having enjoyed bikes."

"I watched them a couple of times, but I'm not really into TV much."

"What about watching them live?" Nash asked.

Joshua lowered his head, looking at his hands. "Never been."

"Really? I love going. We have a great local fair that has a monster truck show, smash-up derby, tractor pulls, the whole nine yards. Even a world-class motocross."

Joshua tilted his head up and looked at Nash. "I would never have pegged you for a smash-up derby or monster-truck kind of guy."

"Why is that?"

"I don't know, I guess I figure it's a redneck kinda sport."

Nash laughed. "Yes, well. I find them fun. Most of my friends don't share my enjoyment in them. I have a hard time finding anyone to go with me. Maybe you'd like to go? It starts at the end of next month."

"Wow, none of your friends like going? I'd love to but never had the opportunity."

Nash gave him a little squeeze. "Then it's a date. Okay, your turn."

"My turn for what?"

"I'm sure you have questions about me. Here's your chance."

Joshua went back to looking at his hands. He was quiet for so long Nash wasn't sure he was going to speak. But finally, without looking up, Joshua asked, "Do you like pets?"

"Yeah. I had a dog, a Mountain Feist, Zoey, but she passed away last year. Haven't had the heart to get another pet yet."

"I'm sorry to hear that," Joshua said, sounding sincere. "I've never had one."

"Oh, they are great dogs. They are actually bred for squirrel hunting. Zoey would watch them from the window, bark and growl, but when I opened the door, she was, like, *no fucking way*. She'd give me this look like she was saying 'You can't expect me to go outside with those wild animals out there.'"

"She sounds great, but I meant I never had a dog," Joshua clarified. "Always wanted one, but never had the chance."

"Would you like to have one?"

"Maybe one day. It's kind of hard to have a dog when you don't have your own place or any money to feed it."

Ah, now it became clear what was weighing down on Joshua's pretty little head. "I know we talked about it, but are you sure you wouldn't prefer to have a job outside of your duties here? Maybe a part-time one?"

Joshua looked up at Nash from beneath his long lashes, a peculiar expression on his face. After a couple of seconds, he shook his head, and when he spoke, he was back to being submissive. "No, Sir. Right now I'd prefer to take care of you. That is, if it's okay with you?"

Nash kissed him on the head. "It's absolutely okay with me. The way I see it, if I had to hire a cook, a housekeeper, gardener, pay for laundry service, and a companion, it would cost me a fortune. Hell, Joshua, I don't think I could afford to pay you what you're truly worth. Are you willing to take out some of it in trade?"

"Wow, when you put it that way…." Joshua left the rest of it hanging as he began to laugh. The sound of his happiness caused Nash's chest to tighten and he couldn't help but laugh as well.

For now, Nash was glad Joshua wouldn't be seeking work outside the home. They really did need the extra time to establish their relationship and get to know each other better. Joshua being gone to work eight to ten hours a day wouldn't be conducive to the type of relationship they were building. They'd reevaluate later. Malcolm was always looking for new help, or maybe Nash would eventually talk Joshua into taking a few classes. It had to be hard to be completely dependent on someone you barely knew. Giving Joshua skills outside his role as submissive, hirable skills, would go a long way in boosting his confidence, Nash was sure.

Chapter Twelve

IGNORING THE urge to slam the phone, Nash set it back on the cradle without smashing the damn thing and sat back in his chair. He was so fucking irritated.

He'd been doing his job for years and had a great reputation for making others money—a lot of money. So why the fuck did someone hire a professional if they weren't willing to listen to his suggestions? In the past few hours, he'd been questioned by one client after another: one complained about his stocks dropping half a point, another questioned the soundness of Nash's predictions, still another bitched about the size of his portfolio even though the asshole had refused to put additional money into it over the past five years. Nash was good at his job, but he wasn't a fucking magic maker.

He pushed up out of his chair and stomped from one side of the room to the other. He was more than irritated; he was totally fucking pissed off. During a typical month, he might get someone complaining about the market—totally understandable. Nash didn't mind explaining the nature of stocks, trends, etc. But every now and then, like today, he got assaulted by stupid questions and bitchy people to an extent that tested his reserves of patience.

He headed for the kitchen, his steps heavy and muscles stiff with irritation. He needed a drink or a fuck or… something to lighten his foul mood. He found something in the kitchen that was sure to help him with his problem.

Joshua was standing at the island, flour scattered across the counter as he rolled out the dough. Some of the white stuff was smeared across his brow and another glob was on his chin.

"Wow, I didn't realize cooking created such a mess." Nash meant for it to be a tease but his foul mood caused his tone to come out sounding stern.

Joshua jerked, his head snapping up and a distressed expression on his face. "I'm sorry, Sir. I get a little carried away when I bake. I'll clean it up."

"I didn't mean to sound so harsh. I was only teasing." Nash moved up behind Joshua, laid a reassuring hand on his arm, and looked over Joshua's shoulder. "What are you making?"

"I'm making bread." Joshua tilted his head, brows dipping low. "Is something wrong, Sir?"

"Wrong? No, there's nothing wrong, except I've been dealing with rude people all morning with stupid questions and people who think I can pull money out of my ass and others who have some crazy fucking notion that they can turn a single dollar into millions." Nash went to the fridge and yanked the door open, snatched up a bottle of water, and twisted off the cap. Before taking a drink, he added, "They don't need an advisor, they need to play the goddamn Powerball lottery." He glanced at Joshua, who had gone back to kneading the dough, arm muscles flexing and rolling, his body swaying slightly with each movement. Damn, he should bend Joshua over the counter and fuck him through it. Relieve a little stress in that sweet, tight ass.

"Anything I can do to help, Sir?"

"As a matter of fact, there is." Nash met Joshua's concerned gaze. "I think you should finish up what you're doing here and meet me in my room."

"Of course, Sir." Those green eyes were shining.

Fuck, the seductive smile curling Joshua's lip caused Nash's dick to harden. "If I were you, I wouldn't have anything in the oven when you come to me. I'd hate to see all your hard work go up in smoke. This is going to be a very lengthy... problem-solving session."

"The dough needs time to rise before I can put it in the oven anyway." The dough might need time, but Joshua certainly didn't. His sweatpants were already tenting.

"Get moving, then." Nash turned on his heel but stopped at the door, a new plan forming in his head. "Meet me in the playroom in five."

Nash headed downstairs, his muscles no longer tense and jerky and his steps easy and measured. Nash inspected the room, going through his cupboards while finalizing his plan. After shoving a condom and a packet of lube in his pocket, he went to check the temperature since the room was a bit stuffy. He turned up the air conditioner and switched on one of the wall fans. After one last look around the room to make sure everything in it was perfect, he nodded to himself.

Joshua entered the room right on time, having washed the flour from his face and looking as excited as Nash felt.

"Strip." Nash was horny, and ready to set the rest of his day on a better track than the bullshit way it had begun.

Joshua pulled his shirt over his head and folded it neatly. He gave the same care to his sweatpants. His motions were smooth, unhurried, controlled. It was as if Joshua knew the best way to deal with Nash at the moment was to remain calm. Oh, but that wouldn't last long. It was about to get hot and heavy, bodies about to get tense and sweaty, and only then would he settle for calm. Already a fire burned in his belly, his nerves tingling.

Nash licked his lips. He opened his pants and freed his cock. "Suck me."

"Yes, Sir." Joshua's tone was soft, his body relaxed as he approached slowly.

Nash's prick twitched in anticipation. There was something extremely erotic about being fully dressed while Joshua was naked, and that he would kneel for him simply because Nash demanded it took it to a whole new level. In a graceful motion, Joshua went to his knees, clasped his hands behind his back, and parted his lips, taking Nash's cock deep. The warm, wet mouth, the slide of tongue, the sudden suction was enough to make Nash's legs shake.

Groaning, he slid his hands along Joshua's stubbled jaw, loving the way his cheeks hollowed beneath Nash's palm. The pleasure skittered along Nash's spine, the warmth of it spreading throughout his body and chasing the aggravation and irritation away. And just like that, Joshua grounded him, eased him.

"That's it, boy. Suck me. Take it all." Nash thrust his hips, loving the way Joshua opened for him, allowing Nash to push deep into his throat.

That talented mouth worked Nash's prick, lips sliding over the shaft and sealing around the base, the suction growing stronger. Nash moved his hand around to the back of Joshua's head, threading his fingers through Joshua's hair, enjoying the way the silky strands tickled across his palm. He didn't need to guide—Joshua knew exactly how to work him, give him what he needed. Oh fuck, how Joshua knew. Each stroke of tongue, each ghost of teeth along sensitive skin, the way he took Nash deep into that tight throat pushed Nash closer and closer.

Nash's balls drew up tight, a knot forming at the base of his spine. "Oh fuck yeah! Close."

Nash pressed his fingers hard against Joshua's skull, holding him still as Nash thrust, short and quick movements, stabbing into that sweet mouth. Joshua took it all. Took every fucking thing Nash gave him with enthusiasm. Nash groaned, the sound rumbling up from deep within his chest when Joshua slid his hand up and cupped Nash's sac, rolling the balls within. It was all the push Nash needed. He gritted his teeth to keep from roaring as he emptied his release down Joshua's throat in long pulses. His body shuddered as the last drop was pulled from him.

Joshua let Nash's cock slip from his mouth and ran his tongue over his lips as if he were looking for more of Nash's flavor. He licked Nash's dick clean, the soft slide of tongue careful but almost too much for Nash's overly sensitive flesh.

Nash patted Joshua's head, panting just a little. "Thank you, boy. I needed that." His balance was restored, the irritation of the morning sucked right out of him—literally—leaving him feeling calm and relaxed.

"You're welcome, Sir. It's my pleasure to service you." Joshua tucked Nash's dick back into his slacks carefully before easing up the zipper and fastening the button.

"I appreciate your willingness to serve me. In fact, you deserve a reward. Go to the wall and choose something." Joshua had eased him, and it was Nash's turn to return the favor.

Joshua rolled to his feet, his cock straining, standing up needy and proud. Nash took a moment to admire that beautiful body, the way it moved as he strolled across the room, head high and shoulders back.

Joshua's body was perfection. Nash's cock twitched, making a gallant effort to fill again. Soon enough, it would. With Joshua's sounds, the heat of his flesh, and appealing scent, how could it not?

Joshua stood with his back to Nash, feet shoulder width apart, hands clasped behind his back, his long black hair cascading down over his shoulders as he stared at the wall. Nash was curious as to what Joshua was thinking. He'd have thought, given what others had told him, that Joshua would instantly pick the long bullwhip. But once again they were wrong about Joshua. Nash would be wise to put out of his head every rumor about Joshua and go on what he knew, or use his instincts and listen to his gut. Joshua didn't choose the whip, cane, or other implements that would have easily broken skin even if Nash held back on the strength of his swings. Joshua took a couple of steps and took the studded paddle from its hook. The paddle was heavy and strong, and it would not only produce a good thud, but the rivets would add a bite.

Joshua came to stand before Nash, then went to his knees, presenting the paddle to him.

Nash accepted it. "Would you prefer to be bound and stretched out on the cross or bent over the spanking bench?"

"I have no preference. It is your pleasure that matters, Sir."

Nash was giddy with pride. Joshua was easily handing him the reins, but it wasn't a robotic response, he could hear the honesty in his tone. *Fuck, I'm a lucky man.* "On the bench."

The bench was equipped with leather restraints attached to the four legs, but Nash wouldn't be binding him. Joshua would have his order not to move to hold him to the bench. If he was truly putting Nash's pleasure before his own, then he would obey. Besides, Nash had learned the night before if Joshua had something else to concentrate on in addition to processing the pain, it took a greater effort on his part and he wouldn't need the extremes he had been pushed to in the past. Such a simple solution, yet efficient.

Nash slapped the paddle against his thigh, testing its weight. "Make yourself comfortable. Once you are in the position, you will not be allowed to move again, nor will you come without my permission."

"Yes, Sir." Joshua lay on the bench, feet planted on the ground, thighs spread slightly. His ass was at just the right level and his heavy balls were exposed.

Nash moved up close and brushed a single finger down Joshua's spine, across his taut ass, then ever so lightly across his sac. He was rewarded with a soft moan. "Mmm… very nice."

Joshua remained silent, his head turned to the side, his expression relaxed. Yet, the flush of color was a testament to Joshua's excitement.

Nash took a couple of deep, centering breaths. He also allowed Joshua's anticipation to grow. After several seconds, Nash placed his left hand in the center of Joshua's back. It was the only warning he gave before bringing the paddle down across Joshua's ass. Joshua didn't move, didn't jerk, but his flesh turned a lovely shade of pink and his muscles tightened.

Nash landed another swat in the same spot, the heavy slap loud in the otherwise silent room. Joshua clenched his ass, but once again it was the only outward appearance that he'd felt the blow. Nash's next swing had the paddle connecting to flesh just below the previous hit and the next to the top of Joshua's thighs. Each thud of leather to skin sent a reverberation up Nash's arm.

Joshua tensed and held his breath for a few heartbeats, and when he let it out, a small pleasure-filled sound escaped with it.

"That's it, let it out. Let me hear your pleasure," Nash encouraged. He landed another blow—harder this time—the force of it pushing Joshua up the bench slightly.

Joshua wrapped his hands around the legs of the bench to keep from being shoved up further, but only made a grunt in response to the paddle.

"Obey me, boy. I want your sounds. Give them to me."

Joshua tightened his jaw and Nash wondered if he was going to follow the command. But then he swallowed hard and replied, "Yes, Sir."

Joshua hesitated just long enough to plant a seed of doubt before he finally agreed. Nash wasn't having it. Joshua would obey, he'd make sure of it. He aimed the blow low on Joshua's ass so that it would clip the top of his balls.

"Ah." Joshua groaned deep and husky, his entire body tensing for a moment.

It wasn't the sound Nash wanted, but it was something, the boy doing as he was told. But Nash wanted more. Wanted the room filled with cries, begging, and screams. He would have it.

He hit the same spot again.

Joshua grunted. It was louder this time, deep and throaty, but still not enough.

Nash brought down the paddle swiftly, with less weight behind the swing, over and over until he got what he wanted.

"Oh fuck! So good…. So…." A blow that hit Joshua's balls stole his words, caught in that perfect second, all tense and breathless before he could speak again. "So good to me, Sir."

"Give me your submission, your mind, and your body, and I can take you places you've never been before." Nash continued to pepper Joshua's ass with quick, sharp blows. The pain wouldn't be in the weight of the slap, but the sheer number of blows.

"Want to go there, want—" Joshua's voice caught on a sob.

"Yes," Nash murmured. With the hand resting on Joshua's back, he dug his blunt fingertips in, enjoying the way his muscles flexed with each swat.

"Want you, so hard, Sir." Joshua's eyes fluttered closed, a look of sheer bliss on his face.

"Close?" Nash inquired without slowing his arm.

"Not yet, Sir. But I can feel each blow in my balls. They're aching, full." Joshua's voice was thick, husky, full of need and want and so fucking sexy it made Nash's dick hard and his toes curl.

Nash's arm began to tire, the muscles shaking with exhaustion. He slid the hand he had on Joshua's back down his spine to his abused ass, feeling the heat, giving his arm a bit of a rest but still giving Joshua the painful sensation he desired. "God, your ass looks so good. All red and the heat. Fuck, Joshua, the heat is incredible. Feels so good against my palm." He went to his knees at the end of the bench and set the paddle down so he was able to take Joshua's ass in both his hands. Then, without warning, he leaned down and put his teeth to Joshua's right cheek, biting hard but not enough to break the skin.

Joshua cried out, the sound raw and rough. His body was trembling and tense as if he was battling to stay put, fighting instinct to pull away from the stinging pain.

Nash bit him again, pulling another howl from his boy, the sound sending a jolt of pleasure straight to his cock, making it twitch and swell impossibly harder.

Nash sat back on his calves, working Joshua's ass with his hands again, scraping his fingernails over sensitive flesh while he spoke. "God, you should see your ass. The way it flexes and rolls. The deep red color. It really is quite the work of art."

"The art would be yours," Joshua groaned, panting a little.

"Yes, but it would be nothing without this lovely canvas." He squeezed Joshua's ass again, emphasizing his meaning.

Nash took in his work, the firm lean body in front of him, his prick twitching again in appreciation of the beauty laid out before him. He pressed a kiss to Joshua's lower back, patted his ass, and then stood. "Roll over."

The bow of Joshua's back, the sweet hiss that passed his lips when he rolled and his abused flesh came in contact with the bench was a thing of beauty, as was the hard and ruddy cock bobbing against Joshua's flat stomach.

"That's it," Nash praised. "Now hook your hands behind your knees and pull them up to your chest."

Joshua did as he was told. He gritted his teeth when the new position put added pressure on the top of his ass. "Like this, Sir?"

"A little tighter. I want that sweet ass exposed."

Joshua shifted, pulling himself into a ball until his ass was lifted up off the bench, putting it and those tight balls on display for Nash.

"Mmm…. Makes my fucking mouth water," Nash moaned, that tight little hole right there. He bent and picked the paddle back up, this time in his left hand.

Nash positioned himself on the other side of Joshua, laid his right hand on Joshua's calf, and began to paddle Joshua's ass in earnest.

Each stroke got Nash a grunt, a groan, a plea, or when the edge of the paddle clipped Joshua's balls, Nash was rewarded with a cry of pain. Soon enough, Joshua was moaning and shaking, fucking dancing for Nash. One well-placed swat had Joshua screaming, tears leaking from the corners of his eyes. At this point, most men would be begging for Nash to stop or would have already used their safeword. But not Joshua. His knuckles were white where he held his knees, and he was sobbing and shaking and yet still rocking into each blow. Nash doubted he could break Joshua with blows to the thick muscles on Joshua's ass. Perhaps he could break him quicker if he aimed for that delicate sac, but he had no desire to damage his boy. One more hard hit on Joshua's ass and then Nash dropped the paddle, letting it fall to the floor with a loud thud.

Nash went back to his knees and spread his hands out against Joshua's thighs, pushing, bending Joshua nearly in half. Before Joshua could catch his breath, Nash leaned down and ran the flat of his tongue along the crease of Joshua's ass and then licked and lapped at the tight little hole.

Joshua bore down as Nash stabbed his tongue into him over and over. Joshua bucked, jerked, and cried out when Nash nipped at the sensitive bundle of nerves. Nash did it again, pulling more sounds from his boy, more movement, just fucking more until Nash was aching, balls heavy and wanting.

Without taking his mouth from Joshua's sweet hole, Nash released one of Joshua's legs and scrambled to find the lube and condom he'd stored in his pocket. He set them next to himself. "Hold that ass up," Nash demanded, growling a little. He released Joshua's other thigh and, without warning, shoved the index finger of his left hand to the hilt into Joshua's spit-slick hole. "Fuck yourself on it."

As Nash undid his pants and freed his cock one-handed, Joshua rocked and thrust, fucking Nash's finger with short quick movements, that tight channel clamping down on Nash's finger, trying to pull it deeper inside him. Nash gave him more, in the form of a second finger, spreading them, stretching the tight muscles, readying it for Nash's fat cock. With difficulty, Nash got the condom on one-handed. As soon as he had it rolled down his shaft and slicked up, Nash surged to his feet, returned his grip on Joshua's thigh, and shoved his cock deep into Joshua's body with one hard thrust.

"Fuck!" Joshua howled.

Nash bit back his groan as the tight, hot hole clenched around his cock and pulled him in deeper, but he couldn't hold back his body.

He tightened his grip on Joshua, hips thrusting, breaching Joshua over and over. Each time his groin made contact with the heated, swollen flesh of Joshua's ass, it made his fucking toes curl and Joshua moan, the sound turning into a jumble of meaningless words with each thrust, the tone like a prayer, a plea.

Nash adjusted his angle. He searched for Joshua's gland. It took a few thrusts, but the sharp cry echoing around the room let Nash know he'd found it.

"Yes! That's it. Right. Fucking. There, Sir. Oh…. Oh fuck, yes."

Nash stayed right there, nudging Joshua's gland again and again. The sweat-slick flesh beneath Nash's hands was hard to keep a hold on, but he dug his fingers in, refusing to release him, slow his thrusts, or change position.

"Don't you dare come," he reminded Joshua, knowing it was an impossible order to obey but wanting, no, needing to hear that safeword pass Joshua's lips before they came.

"I…." Joshua's head was thrown back, long throat working, mouth opening and closing again and again.

Nash gritted his teeth and redoubled his efforts, pistoning in and out of Joshua, stabbing that sweet spot without mercy. "You are mine, your body is mine to do with what I want. I own it, command it."

Joshua tightened further around Nash, whole body shaking and covered in sweat.

"I can't. Sir, please… Sir… I… I…."

"You are not to come," Nash screamed, slamming in and out of Joshua at a brutal pace. A knot formed at the base of Nash's spine, his balls tight against his body and his heart hammering. Sweat rolled down his temples, breath harsh and panting, and still he slammed into Joshua over and over, refusing to back down. Joshua would either safeword and they would soar with their orgasms, or….

"Fuck! Fuck! Fuck!" Joshua shook so hard, Nash thought he might just very well shake apart. Then the dam broke. "Red! Oh god, Sir. Red. Red. Red. Red." Joshua sobbed pitifully.

A gift given, Nash froze for a split second, letting Joshua know he'd heard him. Nash hit the release on the cock ring and at the same time said, "Come. Come now—I want to feel you on my cock."

"Yes. Thank you, thank you, Sir." Joshua's release shot from his hard prick, landing on his neck and chest.

Joshua's body milked Nash's cock, calling out his own orgasm. Without taking his gaze from Joshua's face, Nash let out a low groan and a whisper of Joshua's name. He filled the condom deep inside his boy, wishing they weren't separated by latex. He wanted to mark the inside of his boy as thoroughly as he had the outside and as completely as Joshua had left his mark on Nash's heart.

Chapter Thirteen

DESIRE, CONFUSION, longing all battled each other for supremacy, leaving Joshua shaking and a little unsteady on his feet. He leaned his forehead against the cool glass of the window as the war inside his heart and head raged. How in the hell had he gotten here? No connections, no emotions, and no complications, that had been his motto. Yet here he stood staring out into an empty, lonely nightscape. For a moment, his desire and longing for Nash moved to the forefront as Nash's face flashed in Joshua's mind. A brilliant smile stretched wide across Nash's face. The smile was like a match to a torch, heating him. God, Nash was so gorgeous, so very sexy, so kind, so—Joshua sighed—not the type of man he was used to. He'd never met anyone like him, so different, difficult, complex, and yet everything he'd ever hoped a Dom would be. But it was that smile, that magnificent, happy smile Joshua had witnessed on Nash's handsome face that touched something foreign deep inside Joshua, and for a moment, he lost himself in the pleasure that smile elicited. For a split second, all the confusion and pain melted away, and Joshua couldn't help but smile in return. Then, like dark clouds swallowing up the sun, Nash's face morphed, swirled unidentifiably for a moment, and it was no longer Nash's face, but Corbin's snarling face. Pain, raw and consuming, ripped through Joshua, causing his knees to buckle, and he had to reach out and grab the windowsill to keep from falling.

"You disgust me, you worthless piece of shit."

Joshua shook his head, trying to dispel the image of his previous master, but it did no good, continuing to haunt him, Corbin's angry voice whispering in Joshua's ears.

Worthless.

Stupid.

Pathetic.

Joshua inhaled deeply, struggling to find some calm. He was standing here in Nash's home, in his own room. He had food and a warm bed, and Nash wasn't looking at him with disgust. *You're not locked in a room. You're not hungry. Not bleeding nor is anything broken. You're free. You're here. Just breathe.*

Rolling his shoulders to try to release some of the tension, Joshua took in another deep breath and began to hum, drowning out Corbin's whispers and focusing on the here and now.

Man, he'd been through some shit in his day, but for some strange reason, the situation he found himself in currently was messing him up worse than anything else. Not only was Corbin haunting him more frequently, but one minute he was ready to bolt, the next to stay. He also struggled with following orders and seeing how far he could push the man. What they'd done together was, for the most part, satisfying, especially the paddling and fucking the night before, but even when his body was tired, his dick satisfied, there was still a hole that went unfulfilled.

There had always been a part of him that remained empty, and he couldn't remember a time when he hadn't been searching for something to complete him. He'd never found it. Never would.

He'd been born fucked-up, grew up fucked-up, and would remain fucked-up until there was nothingness. Why in the hell did he keep searching for the impossible?

"Because you're fucked-up," he grumbled, disgusted at himself. He turned from the window and flopped back on the mattress, arms stretched over his head. He ground his ass against the sheets, but the tickling of pain on his red ass wasn't enough to focus on. He ran the fingers of his left hand softly over the thin scars on his right forearm. It had been a long time since they had been etched into his flesh, a couple of years since he'd added to the web of lines. Maybe it was time....

He'd been fifteen, living on the streets, alone, hopeless when he'd experienced his first panic attack. *Christ, had it been ten years ago already?* Ten years and he was still alone and hopeless, only now he could add broken, stupid, and pathetic to the list. Maybe it was time to stop fighting the inevitable. If he could just relieve a little of that ugliness inside him. The first time had been... euphoric.

He sat with his back against the harsh brick wall at the end of a dark alley, the stench of rotting food, vomit, and piss surrounding him, covering him. He was exhausted. All he'd wanted to do was sleep. He didn't even care about the cramping in his stomach anymore if only he could find somewhere warm and dry to sleep. Somewhere safe.

Joshua started to push to his feet when a wave of nausea ripped through him, bile rising up in his throat, burning it. He fell back down onto his ass, shaking so fucking hard he couldn't stand. His heart pounded painfully and made him so dizzy he couldn't see, couldn't think straight. Something was wrong, but he had no idea what it was. It couldn't be food poisoning; he hadn't eaten for over twenty-four hours. Plus, he'd experienced that shit before, and this was different. Not only was his heart racing, but his lungs were also seizing up. He couldn't take in a full breath, only pant while he was filled with a sense of dread. Sheer terror overwhelmed him, his vision going black around the edges—but of what?

A loud bang echoed through the alleyway, an animal hissed, and Joshua jerked. With trembling fingers, he grabbed for his knife. He scanned the area around him wildly, still gripped by fear, unable to flee. Unable to fucking breathe.

The cold metal dragged across the skin of his arm, and suddenly, Joshua was filled with an enormous sense of relief. He looked down at the three-inch wound. There was no pain, the blood sliding down his arm and dripping onto his pants incidental. His breathing slowed, as did his pulse, a calm washing over him, leaving him feeling lighter than he had been in a very long time. He leaned his head back against the brick wall, held his arm up, and continued to stare at the cut, deliriously happy. Finally something that made him feel better—alive.

Joshua jerked to an upright position, breathing harshly as he dug his fingers into his forearm. *No! I will not! No, no, no!* He couldn't, wouldn't go back there. Three years he'd sliced and diced, trying to fill that emptiness inside him, to feel something. The high he'd gotten from it went from lasting for hours, sometimes days, to minutes, then seconds. He'd traded one pain for another the day he walked into his first BDSM club.

Jesus!

Joshua scrubbed his hands over his face. He was beyond deviant; he was truly and utterly disturbed. Again the question of whether he should stay or go reared up. The longer he mulled it over, the more he knew he should leave, because he was having a hard time understanding not only Nash, but himself. But what about the contract? If he broke it, where would he go? Back to the streets?

Not finding any answers within, Joshua pushed to his feet so he could shower and start his day. He stood beneath the flow of hot water, letting it ease his tense muscles. He didn't need to make a decision at this very moment. He'd always rushed into everything without thinking, afraid to think too deeply for fear of unwanted memories crushing him. If it made his dick hard, that was the direction he would take. And now here he was, twenty-five years old, no money, no education, no goals beyond making it through a day that was set out for him, begging, hoping that by the end of it, he'd be taken out of his head and allowed to float free, if only for a moment.

The water turned cool, and he rushed to wash up before the hot water was completely gone. He didn't make it, a blast of cold water sent a shiver ripping through him, and he fumbled to get the taps turned off. He snatched a towel up, wrapped it around his shoulders, and used the ends of it to vigorously rub away the goose bumps that had bloomed along his arms.

Joshua shook his head. Another bad decision he'd made, but one he could easily change.

He pointed at his reflection. "No more thinking in the shower."

NASH WAS pulled gently from sleep, and this time, he knew exactly what it was that had him stretching, a grin on his face. *Coffee.* The scent of the rich brew always woke him, but rather than the programmable pot, it was a handsome, hard body getting his morning caffeine ready for him. It had only taken a couple of days and already he was getting used to having another person in his home. Not just any person but his boy. His Joshua.

His smile grew as the events of the night before came rushing back. Joshua had broken for him. Only the second time taking Joshua to the playroom and he'd submitted beautifully. He'd followed every command, every order without question. He'd found his subspace with ease and he'd done the one thing Nash thought he'd have to wait weeks, perhaps months for—used his safeword. Nash couldn't help but feel a bit smug. He'd suspected Kirk and Troy simply hadn't known how to handle such a precious gift as Joshua, and now he had proof. Joshua didn't need torn flesh and ugly scars to reach that sweet place that made him fly. He was complex and needed dual sensations. He needed not only a stern master and strong hand, but patience and kindness. Soft touches, kisses, warmth. He needed to belong. That no one had figured that out before surprised Nash and pissed him off. So much unnecessary trauma.

A morning chill caused Nash to shiver, and he pulled the covers up to his chin. Tonight Joshua would be in his bed. Waking to coffee was great, but waking to a warm body wrapped around his would be even better.

Nash closed his eyes, the soft mattress and comforter surrounding him, and he started to drift back off to sleep as he waited for Joshua.

The next time he opened his eyes, the room was flooded with sunlight. He looked over toward the side of the bed, but there was no Joshua kneeling next to it and no coffee on the bedside table. Nash frowned at the clock. It was after eight, where in the hell was Joshua?

He slid from the bed, took a quick piss, then headed for the kitchen in search of his boy and his caffeine. The kitchen was empty, no sign of Joshua and no cooling breakfast. The only scent in the room was the bitter aroma of burnt coffee. Irritated, he poured out the wasted brew and refilled the carafe with fresh water.

"Joshua?" Nash called out as he continued to set a new pot to brew.

Once he had the coffee going, he headed down the hall and rapped his knuckles on the spare room door. "Joshua?" Nash waited for a second and, when there was no reply, pushed the door open. He'd expected to find that Joshua had done the same thing Nash had and simply fallen back to sleep, but the room was empty, bed made.

What the hell? Nash rubbed at his sleepy eyes and scratched his hand over his stomach. Irritation quickly turned to alarm when he didn't find Joshua in his bathroom, the safe room, or the living room.

He even checked the playroom, not really surprised when he didn't find Joshua there.

After checking the entire house, Nash headed back to the kitchen to search for a note or some indication of where Joshua had gone. He found nothing and that Joshua's shoes were still sitting by the front door only added to the puzzle. There was only one other place he could check. He grabbed a to-go cup, filled it with a fresh cup of coffee, and headed out the back door.

"Whoa!" Nash exclaimed when he nearly tripped over Joshua, who was sitting on the back steps.

Joshua caught him, steadying him before he could fall down the stairs.

"Thanks," Nash muttered and took a seat next to Joshua on the top step. "I've been looking for you." He held up his mug. "Had to make my own coffee."

Joshua stared at the mug, brows dipping. "I made coffee. Sorry I didn't bring it to you. I needed to get some air."

There was a moroseness to Joshua's voice that tugged at Nash's heartstrings. He didn't comment further on the condition of the coffee Joshua had made or about the fact that he had broken Nash's rules. "How long have you been out here?"

Joshua turned his head and stared out toward the back of the property. "Not that long. I don't think so anyway. I've been kind of preoccupied this morning. What time is it?"

"It's after eight."

"Oh shit!" Joshua started to jump up, but Nash grabbed his arm. "I've got to start breakfast."

"It's okay, I'm not hungry yet. I'd rather you sit with me while I have my coffee."

Joshua hesitated, muscles tense like he was ready to bolt. After a few uncomfortable seconds, he finally slumped back down. He laid his forearms on his knees and hung his head. "Sorry about breakfast."

"Stop apologizing. I'd rather hear what is so heavy on your mind that you lost the last hour or more of time."

"Staying or going," Joshua muttered, his voice so low Nash barely heard him.

"Excuse me?" He needed to be sure he'd heard Joshua correctly.

Joshua stayed so quiet, scarcely breathing, Nash began to wonder if he was going to answer. There was no relief for Nash when Joshua finally responded—"I can't decide if I should stay here or run."—confirming Nash hadn't heard him wrong.

"Was it something I've done? Something here you're not happy with?"

"No…. Well…." Joshua shook his head. "No, not really."

"That doesn't sound all that convincing."

Still not making eye contact with Nash, Joshua said, "It's not you, I don't think, since I'm having a hard time figuring you out and it's messing with my head. Whenever I have to think too much, shit gets weird. I start…. Never mind."

"Start what?" Nash urged.

"I just don't like thinking too much about things is all."

"I get that, but I think it's important that we talk about what you're feeling and thinking."

Joshua's head snapped to the side, and he glared at Nash, eyes blazing. "And I don't fucking like it when people keep asking me what I'm thinking."

The sudden outburst and the venom in his tone took Nash back for a second, and he could only stare at Joshua in complete shock, but he recovered quickly. "I suggest you change your tone of voice when speaking to me. I have no problem allowing you some leeway when you're upset, but you will not curse me, scream at me, or disrespect me, is that understood?"

Joshua continued to stare at him, his expression angry, his body coiled so tightly it looked as if he could break apart at any second. Nash kept his cool, forcing his expression to remain neutral yet firm. He had no idea what the hell had happened between last night and this morning to send Joshua into such a state, but he'd be damned if he was going to allow the man to treat him in such a way, regardless of what had taken place during the night.

Joshua was the first to back down, but not in the way Nash had expected. Suddenly there were tears streaming down Joshua's flushed cheeks, and he was visibly shaking.

"Hey, what's going on?" Nash quickly wrapped Joshua in a tight embrace. "Talk to me."

Joshua shrugged Nash off, and for a heartbeat Nash thought he was going to run. Instead Joshua held out his forearms, palms turned up. "This is what is going on in my head. This is what happens when I have to think too much."

Nash had seen the numerous fine scars on Joshua and assumed they were the result of being improperly bound. Now, with Joshua's words floating through his mind, Nash saw the multitude of scars for what they really were. "Did you do this?" Nash ran a finger over Joshua's right forearm and looked up at him. "Did you cut yourself?"

Joshua nodded, and Nash's heart broke.

Chapter Fourteen

NO MATTER how much Joshua wished otherwise, he couldn't take back what he'd said. As much as he hated that he'd blurted out what was running around inside his stupid thick skull, it was nowhere near how much he despised the look of pity in Nash's eyes.

Joshua wiped away his foolish tears from his cheeks, then folded his arms, hiding the marks of his weakness. "It's nothing. It was a long time ago."

"How long?"

"It's been three years." Unable to stand the look in Nash's eyes, Joshua turned away to stare out over the landscape, but that damn look of pity blurred the view.

Nash placed his hand against Joshua's lower back, the touch no doubt meant to be soothing, but his tension made it impossible to relax. In fact, the touch only made him feel worse, but he didn't pull away. He'd made enough of a mess of the morning. Fuck, hadn't he just told himself he was a fool for making decisions without weighing the pros and cons? That he needed to stop thinking with his dick and diving headfirst into shit? And it might not be his dick this time, but he'd still been a fool.

"How old were you when you started?" Nash asked quietly.

"Fifteen."

"Jesus, Joshua. You were a child."

"I beg to differ," he responded curtly. "And I believe most boys that age would disagree with you. You don't become an adult because of the date on your birth certificate." That was certainly true of his upbringing. He'd never been a child, or at least never had a childhood to speak of. He'd been fending for himself pretty much all his life.

"No, I don't suppose my fifteen-year-old self would have thought I was a child either, but I know better now. Did anyone try to get you help to deal with the cutting?"

"Yeah, me. I told you, I haven't done it in a long time, and I'm doing my best not to go there again. That's why it's important not to think, and I'd appreciate it if you didn't ask me to." Joshua was filled with nervous energy, his heart beginning to race. He pushed to his feet, needing to move, to pace, to get the hell away from Nash and this line of questioning. He was an idiot for bringing it up.

"I know you don't want to talk about it, but quite honestly, I think you should. I have a friend who is into the lifestyle who is also a therapist. I'd be happy to introduce you."

"No. I mean, thanks but right now, I don't know if I can handle anyone else asking me what I'm thinking or feeling."

"I really wish you would reconsider. I think it may help."

Joshua shoved his hands in his pockets, continuing to pace back and forth. "I'd rather be taken out of my head. It's a much safer place and there is zero chance I'll need to feel the pleasure of the blade."

"And I'm going to assume this is a deal breaker. That I must agree to take you out of your head and keep you there often or you'll run?"

"Yes."

Nash pushed to his feet and headed up the back stairs. "I'll get our contract and tear it up. You're free to do what you wish."

Joshua stopped dead in his tracks. "That's it?"

Nash turned with his hand on the doorknob. "You agreed to be my submissive and follow my rules. Now you are saying you are making the rules and I must follow them, or you run. I'm more than willing to make sure you have the help you need. However, I refuse to be told what to do." With that, Nash went into the house, the slamming of the screen door causing Joshua to jump.

He stared at the empty back porch, panic skittering down his spine and kicking up his pulse. *Fuck!* Where in the hell was he going to go now? Should he crawl back to Troy? Go back to the streets? Both made his stomach roil. Both options weren't really options at all. He'd thrown the gauntlet down, and it shouldn't surprise him that Nash walked past without picking it up. But if he went back on his word now and allowed things to continue as they were, he'd be cutting again. The thought was both exciting and terrifying. But mostly terrifying.

There was a fourth option. Nash had just offered to make sure he got any help he needed. Joshua wasn't sure he understood what that meant, but as he followed Nash into the house, he held on to that small sliver of hope.

Nash was in the kitchen refilling his coffee mug when Joshua entered. "I'm sorry for the way I put demands on you. I shouldn't have done that, but...." Joshua blew out a heavy sigh. "Actually, I have no fucking clue what to say or what to do," he admitted.

Nash turned and leaned against the counter, coffee mug in hand. "What do you want to do?"

"I don't know. The only things I do know is I don't want to go back to Troy or the streets, I don't want to feel trapped, I don't want...." Joshua ran his fingers through his hair, clasping his hands behind his head and closed his eyes. "God, I just don't fucking know."

"I must say I'm a bit hurt that you didn't say you didn't want to leave me, but that's my ego talking, I'm sure."

Shit! That hadn't come out right. He didn't want to leave Nash, but.... No, there was no excuse for hurting Nash's feelings. Joshua moved up close to Nash and lowered his head. "I didn't mean to hurt your feelings. Of course I want to stay with you, I just don't know if it's the right thing for either of us right now. I'm so fucked up in the head, and it's your kindness that I'm having the hardest time dealing with."

The last thing Joshua expected was for Nash to wrap his arms around him, but that's exactly what he did, holding Joshua tight. "That breaks my heart."

"Please don't pity me, I can't stand it," Joshua begged, but he didn't pull away nor did the anger flare up. He was so fucking tired of thinking, afraid to stay, but too afraid to run. He was a broken coward. "I do want to stay, but I'm afraid of the things I'm feeling." He looked up and met Nash's gaze. "I'm afraid of feeling alive."

NASH CONTINUED to hold Joshua, and he couldn't help the way he was feeling. It was heartbreaking to hear the man talk about his past and it was a pity that it had been so horrible. He couldn't agree to Joshua's terms, nor could he force the man to stay, but Jesus, he didn't want to be just another person in the long list who had failed Joshua. This was Joshua's decision to make. The only thing Nash could do was try to convince him to stay. Perhaps they could come up with a compromise that would be agreeable for them both, or that was it. Nash's dominant nature couldn't bow down to Joshua's demands, and he was sure Joshua wouldn't be able to flourish or heal being the one in charge. They needed time to reevaluate their relationship. Part of Nash believed setting the contract aside and relaxing the rules would be detrimental. But somehow they had to figure out a way to work together in a way in which their natural dispositions could still shine, yet allow an environment in which Joshua could speak freely about his fears.

Nash kissed the top of Joshua's head and then released him. "Let's go have a seat and see if we can come up with a way we can make this work that we both are happy with."

"I'm surprised you're not going to show me to the front door."

"You know where it is and can leave at any time, but I'm hoping you'll at least give us a chance."

"I'd like that." Nash heard the sincerity in Joshua's tone, and he couldn't help but smile in relief.

They sat shoulder to shoulder on the couch, Nash with his coffee and Joshua with his glass of Coke. Nash propped his feet on the coffee table, doing his best to relax, but Joshua stayed rigid. Neither of them said anything, and with each tick of the clock, the anxiety radiating off Joshua increased and filled the space between them until Nash could no longer even feign calm.

"So here—"

"I don't—"

"After you—"

"Sorry, go—"

And just like that, the tension between them burst as they began laughing. Nash laid his hand on Joshua's thigh and, once he had Joshua's attention, said, "I was thinking that we take a week, maybe even two, where we relax a few of the rules. I don't believe we should completely ignore the terms of our contract. However, we do need to spend time getting to know each other better, reevaluating our goals, and then making a clear-cut plan on how to achieve them."

"I don't know, Sir." Joshua turned his head and looked down at his hands. "I don't do very well when left to make my own choices. I'll overthink shit. Thinking and no pain?" Joshua shook his head vigorously. "I can't. I'll end up reaching for the blade. I know I will."

"I can understand that. However, I honestly believe you need time and opportunity to deal with past issues. If I'm telling you what to do and how to feel twenty-four seven, we will be right back to where we are at the moment. I don't want you to question wanting to be here. I also don't want you to ever wonder if I want you here and I damn sure don't want you feeling as if you need to hurt yourself to feel alive. That's my job. *I* want to make you feel alive."

"I don't know if you can," Joshua mumbled.

It didn't surprise Nash that Joshua didn't have faith in him. Trust had to be earned, and given Joshua's past, that was the one thing Nash was sure would be the hardest goal to achieve. Still, he couldn't help but feel a twinge of disappointment.

"If you're not sure of me, why have you suddenly started calling me Sir again? I mean don't get me wrong, I don't mind, but you certainly flip-flop between referring to me that way and then forgetting."

"I…." Joshua tilted his head, clearly thinking about the answer. It took him a couple of minutes, and Nash was glad to see he was putting that much thought into it. "I think part of it may be your fault, Sir."

"How so?"

"In the way you deal with me. Sometimes you treat me as your lover or boyfriend and other times like your submissive. I'm having a hard time understanding what you want from me at any particular moment. I prefer seeing you as my Dom. It's easier for me."

"I can understand that and I don't mean to confuse you. I'm trying to do what I believe is best for both of us, but it's a learning process. Rules are going to change, as our needs do. But I do see you as both my submissive and lover, and one day I also hope to be able to consider you my boyfriend if everything works out between us."

Joshua muttered something so low, Nash couldn't hear him.

"What was that?"

"I've never had a boyfriend before. I don't think I'm boyfriend material."

Nash closed his eyes and tried not to react to the tightening in his chest or the way Joshua's statement tore at his heart. A sickening feeling settled into his gut. The more time he spent with Joshua, the more heartbreaking facts Nash discovered. He honestly believed he couldn't save Joshua by keeping a strict D/s relationship between them. Yet, treating him as Nash's lover was confusing Joshua. Dammit, Nash hated being indecisive. Somehow, he had to figure out how to find a balance. If they kept going the way they started, Joshua wouldn't have to look back or deal with his past, something he so desperately needed to do if he wasn't to end up a broken man. Or worse....

Nash pushed the distressing thought away. He would not fail Joshua and he damned sure wasn't going to give up.

Suddenly, Joshua jumped to his feet. "I can't do this."

"Do what?" Nash pushed to his feet but didn't follow after Joshua as he began to pace.

"I can't be a boyfriend; I can't be your equal."

"Joshua—"

"I can't. I won't. It can only end badly, and I couldn't stand it if you ended up hating me."

"I could never hate you," Nash said gently.

"You say that now. Maybe we should just forget all about this. I think I should just go."

Nash set his coffee mug down and rushed to Joshua, taking his arm and halting his movements. "No. Please don't go. I want you to stay. If you'll just give us a chance, I know we can figure this out."

Joshua stared at him with a hesitant expression, but Nash could see the longing in those beautiful green eyes.

"Please," Nash said softly. "I know you're having a hard time finding your place here. But I'm confident we can make this work." Nash ran a soothing hand up and down Joshua's back. "I think we are worth the chance."

"I've never had anyone beg me to stay," Joshua responded softly, averting his gaze.

"Would you like me to get on my knees to show you how sincere I am? I don't often beg, but I will if it will convince you to stay."

"No, please don't do that, Sir. But it might help if I could understand why you want someone as fucked-up as me to stay."

"Because you may not be able to see it, but I see the good in you. I've known from the instant I first laid eyes on you that I was looking at someone very special." Nash laid his palm gently against Joshua's cheek. "I'm even more convinced my instincts were right. I know I can help you find peace if you'll just give me a chance."

Joshua looked up and briefly met Nash's gaze. He quickly turned away but not before Nash saw the unshed tears in his watery gaze. Nash pulled him into a hard embrace. "I'm not letting you go, Joshua. We will figure this out together."

As Nash held the trembling man, heard the soft sobs he was trying to hide, it only cemented Nash's conviction. He was going to figure out a way to help this poor man. Joshua wasn't broken. He just needed to know someone cared about him. Somehow, they had to figure out how to balance their needs, something that would be much easier if he could break down that wall surrounding the man and figure out a way to crawl into Joshua's head and heart.

Chapter Fifteen

THERE WAS no way they could completely forgo the contract. Joshua might not have cared that boundaries weren't set when Troy shared him, but Nash refused to have a relationship like the one between him and Joshua's without at least some kind of guidelines. After his chat with Joshua, Nash had called Malcolm, whose response was "Are you completely crazy?" And perhaps Nash was, but deciding to take a vacation, and leave the contract at home, would give him and Joshua a couple of days to talk and spend time together on an equal playing field. Once Nash had explained what had transpired between him and Joshua, why they needed the mini time-out, Malcolm was on board and agreed that sometimes unconventional things needed to be tried.

Today they'd be heading south to a small cabin in Monroe, Kentucky. Nash had spent a couple of summers there with his grandparents when he was growing up, but hadn't been in years. From what he'd discovered during his Google search, the town hadn't changed much in twenty years. It was the perfect place to get away and not have anyone to bother them.

While there was no Dom/sub relationship per se, Nash had agreed to Joshua's request for daily spankings. It was something they both enjoyed, so why deny themselves the pleasure. Nash smiled. Once he'd reddened Joshua's ass, he had a surprise for Joshua. Although the man might not be too happy with Nash's gift.

"Joshua, could you come in here for a moment?" Nash called out.

He heard Joshua rattling something in the kitchen and after a few minutes, he popped his head around the doorjamb of Nash's office. "Did you need something, Sir?"

"Did you get the snacks for the trip packed?"

"Yes, Sir. Just finished up."

"Your bag prepared?"

"Yes, Sir."

"Good. Just one more thing to take care of and we'll get on the road. Please have a seat." Nash gestured to the chair opposite him.

Joshua looked wary, but he took the seat. He groaned when Nash held up what he'd been hiding in his hand.

"I take it you know what this is?"

"Yes, Sir, it's a cock cage. I hate those things."

Nash arched a brow. "Bad experience with them?"

"Only if you consider the time Master Corbin left me in one for a full month a bad experience. They can be quite distracting, Sir. Not to mention uncomfortable as hell."

"Only if you get hard."

"I know." Joshua sighed. "Trust me, I know, Sir. My dick has a mind of its own sometimes."

Nash leaned back in his chair, fingers sliding along the smooth plastic. "It's not a bad thing that you dislike them. I'd like to use it on you."

Joshua's brows shot up nearly to his hairline. "What am I being punished for?"

Nash shook his head. "You're not being punished for anything. Rather, I'd like to use it as a tool. With what you've told me about your past with cutting and seeing as you're unwilling to talk to a therapist—against my better judgment, I might add—I'm only willing to concede if you're willing to try something else."

"I'm listening," Joshua said, sounding suspicious.

"I know you get immense pleasure from your morning discipline, and it would be counterproductive to reaching our goals if I was to withhold all pain. What I would like to do is to start working on diminishing some of the pleasure you find in pain, bringing it back from the edge, so to speak, so that you can still enjoy some of the things you like but within limits. You need to relearn how to view pain and pleasure in a healthy environment without it controlling you. I'm also hoping that while we are on our getaway, we'll find other things that make you happy."

Joshua lowered his head, but Nash could see the thoughtful expression on his face.

"Would you like some time to think about it?"

Joshua shook his head, but he didn't respond right away. Nash didn't push, giving Joshua all the time he needed to think about his answer.

Finally, after a couple minutes, Joshua nodded and lifted his head to meet Nash's gaze. "As much as I hate those damn things, if you think it will help, then I'm willing to try, Sir."

Nash smiled; how could he not? The trust Joshua was putting in him was an honor. He hoped with time and a little ingenuity, they'd be able to find a healthy balance in their relationship. If he couldn't curb Joshua's need for pain and cutting, then he'd insist Joshua go into therapy. Hell, hopefully as Joshua became more confident in his life, he'd want to speak with someone to deal with the past abuse issues. It was the only way he was truly going to heal.

"Thank you for trusting me." Nash pushed his chair back. "Come here and drop your pants."

"Yes, Sir," Joshua responded, already pushing down his pants while making his way to Nash.

Nash took a second to appreciate Joshua's neatly shaved groin, slender cock, and heavy balls. He took Joshua's cock in his free hand. He clamped down on his lips, holding back the grin that threatened when Joshua tensed and slightly pulled away from his touch. Nash wasn't cruel; he didn't actually stroke Joshua's prick, no matter how much he wished to do otherwise. As quickly but gently as he could, Nash slid Joshua's cock inside the cage and secured it into place.

"The wide plastic design allows for you to use the bathroom without removing it. I will take it off you at night. I won't make you sleep in it, but it's to go back on first thing in the morning. Is that understood?"

"Yes, Sir."

Nash ran his hand soothingly up and down Joshua's thigh. "Remember, you are not being punished, but it's being used as a means to a goal."

Joshua muttered something, but it was so low Nash couldn't make out what he was saying.

"What was that?"

"Nothing, Sir. I guess it's worth a try."

"Do you not want to try?"

"It's not that."

When Joshua didn't comment further, Nash said, "You've admitted to me that you've been finding pleasure in pain since you were very young. I'm not saying there is anything wrong with enjoying a good ass whipping or allowing pain to set you free and let you soar for a while. But you've let it control your life instead of you controlling it. I'd really like you to try this."

Joshua stared down at the cock cage for a moment before finally letting out a breath and allowing his shoulders to slump. "Yeah, we can try it, Sir. Not going to be a lot of fun, though."

"And neither is cutting yourself," Nash reminded him gently. "You can do this, Joshua. I know you can. I believe in you."

"Thank you, Sir. At least, someone does."

"Sometimes all it takes is for one person to believe. Now, let's redden that ass, shall we?"

Without the normal enthusiasm he showed when it was time for his discipline, Joshua moved into position. He placed his hands on the floor and raised his ass to the right level for Nash. Nash picked up the heavy wooden hairbrush from his desk. It would warm Joshua's ass nicely without the added sting the studded paddle gave. The stinging pain would come from the cage around Joshua's cock as he reacted to the blows.

Nash patted Joshua's buttcheek with his free hand, the only warning he gave before pulling his arm back and landing a hard blow to Joshua's bare ass. The only response from Joshua was a small grunt.

Nash began peppering Joshua's ass with light but steady blows, spreading them out and avoiding hitting the same spot over and over in succession. It wasn't long before Joshua began to pull away slightly, having learned Nash's rhythm and no doubt anticipating the blows. Nash didn't change the weight behind his swings but the time in between them was deliberately erratic. The change got the desired results, and Joshua began to pant, groaning and grunting with each swat.

"No, no, no, no," Joshua muttered. His tone was low, apparently talking to himself rather than Nash.

Nash kept up the erratic rhythm, and it didn't take many more before Joshua said something that was pure music to Nash's ears. "Yellow."

Nash set the brush down and rubbed at the abused flesh, enjoying the heat radiating off Joshua's ass. It was the right thing to do to push Joshua to the edge, the little extra pain broke him. "Red!" Joshua jerked up, going to a standing position. His eyes were squeezed tightly shut, and he was breathing hard.

Nash didn't move, didn't speak, giving Joshua a moment to get himself under control. The skin of Joshua's cock pushed through the small square in the cage as it swelled.

"Would you like me to remove the cage?" Nash asked.

Joshua shook his head. One minute, then another and still Joshua was breathing harshly, eyes closed.

Nash pressed his hand against Joshua's lower back. "Deep breaths. You can do this. I know you can. Just breathe."

A few more tense seconds and Joshua finally sucked in a deep breath and let it out slowly before he opened his eyes. "Okay, that totally sucked, Sir."

"I know, but you did amazingly well. I'm very proud of you."

Joshua seemed to relax further with Nash's praise, and he even found a small smile, which was pretty impressive considering how uncomfortable he had to be. Nash patted his arm. "Okay, let's get the car packed and we'll get on the road."

Joshua winced when he pulled up his pants and spent a couple seconds adjusting them to find a more comfortable spot for his caged dick to lie, but he didn't complain even while stiffly walking out of the room.

Nash had no crazy expectations that this new addition to Joshua's morning discipline would cure him, but it was a start, and when they returned from their trip, he'd work on getting Joshua to agree to see a professional. Nash could deal with the pain issues, he was confident of that. But he wasn't trained in mental health, and nothing he did or said could truly help Joshua deal with the horrors of his past.

THE LANDSCAPE had gone from flat and boring to rolling hills and beautiful. Joshua supposed it didn't matter what the scenery had to offer for the first hour of their trip because he was too focused on his dick to see anything. He loved the slight pain in his ass from the spanking, but that in itself was a problem. Every time he shifted, the pain and heat of his reddened ass would flare to life, and with it, his prick tried to fill.

Fucking cock cages. He leaned his head against the cool glass of the window and swallowed down his sigh.

"I want to make a stop in Lexington and get you some new clothes."

"I don't need any, Sir. You've already been very generous with the ones you've given me."

"I don't want you having to wear my hand-me-downs. You need your own things."

Joshua turned his head to look at Nash, the guilt and embarrassment making his gut roll. "Really, I don't want you spending money on me. I like the clothes you gave me."

"You'll earn every dime I spend on them. This is going to be a wonderful vacation lying back and relaxing. Waking up every morning and getting to redden that ass of yours for me to enjoy looking at while you cook, clean, and wait on me hand and foot."

Joshua cocked his head. "If you plan on watching my ass while I take care of you, what do I need clothes for?"

"Because it makes me happy."

"I—"

Nash laid his hand on Joshua's thigh and squeezed. "Just let me do this for you, please?"

Oh Jesus. How was he supposed to argue with that? Nash glanced over and gave him a pouty look, and there was no way Joshua could refuse. He didn't have to like it—cooking and cleaning for room and board was one thing, but he didn't like Nash throwing money away on him. Still, he nodded. "Okay, if it makes you happy, Sir."

"Ridiculously so," Nash responded with a wide smile and patted Joshua's leg.

When they stepped into a men's shop in the downtown area of Lexington, Joshua was rethinking his agreement. He'd gotten a glance at the sale price on T-shirts and nearly swallowed his tongue. Who in the hell paid thirty dollars for one T-shirt?

"Good afternoon. My name is Kenneth. If I can assist in any way, please let me know," greeted an older gentleman dressed in a tailored suit.

"Hi, Kenneth, as a matter of fact, you can help us out. I'm Nash, and my companion Joshua here"—Nash stabbed a thumb in Joshua's direction—"needs to be measured."

"Wonderful. If you'd like to follow me, I'll show you to the dressing area."

Joshua followed them past a curtain into a room with a couple of leather chairs placed before a trifold of large mirrors.

Kenneth pointed to a wooden box on the floor near the mirrors. "If you'd like to step up on this, I'll grab my tape measure."

Joshua stopped next to Nash and whispered close to Nash's ear. "He's not going to ask me to remove my pants, is he?"

Nash's brows furrowed in obvious confusion, and then Joshua could tell from the smile curling Nash's lip when he figured out what Joshua was talking about. "No, he's not going to get to witness how sexy you look in that cage." Nash pecked Joshua's cheek. "He has no idea what he's missing."

Joshua fought the urge to roll his eyes. The cage was very far from sexy, and he doubted Kenneth would appreciate the view as much as Nash apparently did. Joshua stepped onto the box just as Kenneth rejoined them.

"Arms out," Kenneth instructed. He began taking measurements, moving around Joshua as he continued to speak. "Anything in particular you're looking for?"

"We're going to need a couple pairs of jeans, brown and black dress slacks with shirts to match, as well as a few casual shirts, socks, and underwear." Nash snapped his fingers. "Oh, and he's going to need shoes."

"Very good, sir. As soon as I'm done with the measurements, I will bring you some items to try on."

Joshua gritted his teeth, keeping his mouth shut until Kenneth was finished. As soon as he was done and left the room, Joshua rounded on Nash. "That's too much! I don't need all that."

"It's not a lot, Joshua. The essentials, really, but it's a start."

Joshua crossed his arms over his chest. "I won't let you."

Nash stood in front of Joshua and ran his hand down the side of Joshua's thigh, looking up at him. "What if I told you it would really, really turn me on to see you dressed up or maybe in a pair of tight-fitting jeans."

"No."

"Joshua. This isn't for you, it's for me. I want to take you out, show you off while we're on vacation. I don't mind you wearing my clothes, but they're too big and they deny me the view of your gorgeous body while clothed."

Joshua didn't even try to hold back on the urge to roll his eyes. "For you, huh?"

"Yes."

"Fine, but I plan on paying you back."

"Only if you want to," Nash said easily. He winked at Joshua and went back to one of the leather chairs.

It really was useless to argue with someone as determined and stubborn as Nash. Joshua would pay him back. Somehow. He didn't know how, but he'd figure it out. Maybe he could do some handyman work, clean gutters, or mow lawns. He'd done it when he was younger.

By the time they left, Joshua had his arms full of bags and was a little nauseated at how much he'd have to pay back. *Holy fuck, nine hundred dollars!* Eh, he'd figure it out because the way Nash had looked at him with lust in his eyes as Joshua had modeled the chosen outfits was worth any amount of money.

Chapter Sixteen

JOSHUA WAS worried about the combination of bacon and boy bits. Solution: long canvas apron that just so happened to tie right above a freshly paddled ass.

"You were wrong."

"Excuse me, Sir?" Joshua asked, looking back over his shoulder.

"You said I couldn't have it all, and here you are with that luscious red ass shining while making me bacon. I feel like a fucking king."

Joshua shook his head, laughing as he turned back to the flip his bacon. "You're so weird."

Nash pushed up off of his stool and quietly moved across the kitchen to stand behind Joshua. He waited until Joshua had turned off the burner and set the fork down before grabbing two handfuls of ass.

"Hey!"

Joshua spun around, and Nash grabbed him and pulled him away from the stove and into his arms. "What did you call me?"

"Weirdo," Joshua repeated and pushed up closer still, rubbing a little, teasing.

Nash didn't discourage it. In fact, he took that fine ass back into his hands and kneaded the taut muscles, enjoying the heat radiating off Joshua's flesh. Nash started to hump back; breakfast could wait. Suddenly he wasn't all that hungry. For food, anyway.

In the blink of an eye, Nash went from having an armful of naked and rutting man to reaching out and grasping nothing but air when Joshua spun away. "No, no, no," Joshua chanted and rushed to the fridge.

Nash stood there for a heartbeat in confusion and then burst out laughing when Joshua grabbed a handful of ice and slid it under his apron to his groin. "It's not funny." Joshua scowled and pointed a finger at Nash. "You did that on purpose."

Nash held up his hands. "I swear I didn't."

"Then why are you laughing at my misery?"

Nash clamped his hand over his mouth. "I'm not," he mumbled but was unable to hold back the snort that followed his denial, totally ruining it. He closed the space between them and took Joshua's wrist, pulling his hand from beneath his apron. "How about I make it up to you?"

Joshua tossed the ice cube into the sink. "And just how do you plan to do that?"

Nash smiled and leaned forward to bite at Joshua's neck. He smelled good. He smelled a little like the breakfast he'd been cooking, but he also smelled like the soap he'd washed in and musk and man and so damn delicious, Nash could eat him up.

It had been a couple of days since either of them had gotten off, and they were long overdue. Joshua had been doing so well with the cage, he deserved a little reward. Oh, and Nash needed one too simply for resisting as long as he had. It had been far, far too long.

Without lifting his head, still licking and kissing and tasting, Nash pushed the apron out of the way and carefully removed the cage around Joshua's cock. "How's this?"

"It's a start, Sir."

Nash rubbed at the warm skin of Joshua's belly and dropped his hand lower, taking Joshua's poor abused prick in his hand and shamelessly jerking him off till he began to harden. "Am I getting closer?" Nash teased. Joshua wasn't the only one getting hard.

"Oh yeah," Joshua moaned and pressed his cock into Nash's hand.

Nash grinned, scraping his teeth against the side of Joshua's neck. "God, you're making me so hard."

Joshua boldly reached out and ran his hand up and down the bulge in Nash's pants. "Mmm, very hard indeed, Sir. I think I could help you out with this."

Nash pushed down on Joshua's shoulder. "I want your mouth."

Joshua went immediately to his knees, his breath hot as he mouthed Nash's prick through his pants and his nimble fingers worked open the fly.

Nash curled his hand around the edge of the counter and with the other hand threaded his fingers in Joshua's hair. Joshua stroked him lightly. "More," Nash whispered. "Stop teasing me. Make me feel it."

Joshua complied, tightening his grip around Nash's shaft. He stroked him from tip to base a couple of times before he took the head of Nash's cock into his mouth.

Nash bit down on his bottom lip, watching his cock slide in and out of Joshua's warm, wet mouth. Joshua shifted, and with a sweep of his arm, the apron fell to the side and exposed his own erection. It swayed with each bob of Joshua's head, the sight nearly as erotic as watching him suck cock. Nash tightened his fingers on Joshua's head and thrust a little deeper. "Oh yeah. Just like that. Going to fuck you so hard so—" Nash's breath caught when teeth scraped across sensitive flesh. "—so deep."

Joshua apparently liked the idea. He groaned and teased the underside of Nash's erection with his tongue, sucking hard and taking Nash deep. Joshua's fingers were firm, stroking. Nash knew exactly what Joshua was doing, trying to push Nash to the edge quicker so he would get what Nash promised him that much faster. Joshua moaned again, and his free hand slid into his lap to press against his hard cock.

Joshua wasn't the only one who had tricks up his sleeves. "Do it," Nash demanded. He swallowed, rotated his hips a little, and pushed into Joshua's throat, gritting his teeth against the tight pleasure. He held Joshua's head still before reluctantly pulling back until he slipped from Joshua's mouth. "Stroke your cock. I want to watch."

Joshua took himself in hand, sliding his fingers along his shaft with a soft pleasure-filled sound. He looked up at Nash from under dark lashes and wantonly ran the tip of his tongue around his lip.

"Feels good, Sir," Joshua whispered.

Nash watched for a moment, transfixed by the movement of Joshua's hand, the way it moved along his ruddy shaft, the way the tip of his thumb teased across the flared head on each pass. Nash's own prick twitched and he reached for it, stroking in time with Joshua. "That's it, keeping stroking it," he murmured. Using his other hand, Nash tipped Joshua's head up and guided himself back in, past those sweet lips.

Joshua moaned as Nash filled his mouth again. Joshua's hand slid from Nash's hip to his ass, blunt fingers digging in as he encouraged

Nash to move. Nash obliged him, thrusting lightly in short stabs. Joshua's eyes fluttered closed as he continued making wet sucking sounds, sounds that were like a lightning strike to Nash's growing arousal.

"Oh god," Nash moaned before he could clamp down on it. His pleasure was building, spiraling toward orgasm far more quickly than he thought it would. Joshua was stripping him of control with his wicked, talented mouth. With a groan, Nash pulled away again, taking short panting breaths as he tried to rein in his out-of-control libido.

"Damn, that was close." The sly, knowing grin on Joshua's face was enough to help Nash regain some of his control. "Such a smug little cocksucker. I have a good mind to make you watch me jerk off and leave you needing."

"And deny yourself punishing me, Sir?"

Nash started to respond, but those lust-filled eyes settled on him and.... *Fuck!* He'd repay Joshua for his cockiness in another way. "Hands and knees," he gritted out.

Joshua smiled knowingly, then turned around and rested his hands on the tile floor, red ass in the air for Nash.

Nash went to his knees behind Joshua and rummaged in his pocket. "You're a very naughty boy, aren't you?"

"I'm whatever you want me to be, Sir." Joshua panted a little, evidence of his undeniable excitement. "God, Sir. I hope you want me to be naughty with your dick up my ass."

Nash slapped Joshua on the ass, hard. "Lucky for you it's exactly how I want you," he said tightly. Joshua wasn't the only one who was breathless with anticipation. Nash set the condom on the floor next to him, opened the lube, slicked up his fingers, and slowly pushed two fingers into Joshua's ass. "This what you want, boy?"

Joshua gasped, his body going rigid with the invasion, ass clamping down on Nash's fingers. Nash held still, giving Joshua time to relax. "Feels good, Sir, but not enough. Want your cock. Need you deep inside me, Sir."

How could he deny Joshua? Hell, how could he deny himself such pleasures? It had been a couple of days, which was a feat in itself with Joshua around. Nash's hands were shaking as he rolled the condom on, his need riding him hard, making his movements jerky.

He guided his cock to Joshua's ass, nudged his way into Joshua's body. He was overwhelmed with the need to drive himself deep, his lust raw and animalistic. It took every bit of will to hold back and keep his movements slow and smooth rather than slamming into the tight channel.

"Yes," Joshua hissed. He arched and panted.

"So good, so fucking tight around my cock," Nash praised.

"Love the way you stretch me, fill me. God, Sir, fuck me, please," Joshua begged as Nash sank deep and their bodies pressed together.

Nash rolled his hips, just enjoying the heat of Joshua's red ass against his groin for a moment. He laid his hands on Joshua's ass, spreading his cheeks wide and going a bit deeper before sliding out slowly, watching as the flared head of his cock stretched that tight little hole further before sinking back in to the hilt. "Is this what you want?" he asked, pulling out just as slowly until only his cockhead breached him.

"No, yes, I mean…. Need more," Joshua babbled. He arched and pressed back into Nash, begging with his body. "Please, Sir," he whimpered. "God, please fuck me, Sir. Please!"

"Jesus," Nash groaned when Joshua bore down on his cock. He slid his hands over to tighten around Joshua's hips, and Nash pulled hard, dragging Joshua back onto him at the same time as he thrust forward. "Fuck," he growled, stabbing into Joshua again and again. "Is this what you wanted?"

"Yes!"

"This how you like it? Hard and fast?" Nash snapped his hips, emphasizing his words.

"Fuck, yes!"

Joshua took every stroke of Nash's cock, his tight hole clamping down each time Nash went deep. "You're trembling. Are you close?"

"Yes! Close!" Joshua cried out, the shaking increasing, his body tightening in waves. "So, close Sir!"

Nash's rhythm became erratic as pleasure surged through him. His body was on fire, ignited by Joshua's tight ass, his sounds, his smell. Nash's grip slipped on Joshua's sweat-slicked flesh and he had to dig his fingers in harder to keep his hold on him. He slowed, shortening his strokes, not yet ready to give over to orgasm. Not ready to let it end. It felt too good. He had to hold on a bit longer. Let it build. He panted, gritting his teeth as he fought the demands of his body.

Joshua whimpered pitifully. "No, please. So close...." He panted harshly for a few seconds, just fucking vibrating, sending a tingling sensation racing up Nash's cock and settling into his balls. He sucked in another harsh breath and choked out a needy sound. "Please, Sir."

Nash shut his eyes tight, his hips jerking out of control, sac heavy, aching. "God, what you do to me, boy." He buried himself to the hilt, cock twitching wildly, his release inevitable. "Come for me," Nash demanded.

"Yes! Gonna come.... Thank you, Sir, god!" Joshua was practically sobbing as his ass tightened around Nash's cock seconds before he gave into pleasure.

Nash clenched his jaw, holding his breath as he felt Joshua's orgasm. Only when Joshua whispered, "Oh god," his body slumping slightly, did Nash let go, stepping over the edge, pushing deep, and coming hard into Joshua's heat.

Nash allowed Joshua to hold his weight for a moment before he kissed Joshua's hair and nuzzled him gently. "Now that one hunger has been sated...."

"Ugh, you're not actually going to make me fix breakfast now, are you, Sir? Wouldn't you rather just lie here and snuggle for a while?"

"And be stuck to the cold, hard floor? Not a chance." Nash laughed, then groaned when he slid from Joshua's body. He went to his feet and held out his hand. "Let's get cleaned up and get breakfast before I fall over from hunger."

"Yes, Sir." Joshua winced when he stood, his knees bright red, but he didn't complain.

Nash pressed a soft kiss to Joshua's lips. "After breakfast we'll cuddle up on the couch and watch a movie."

"That's the second-best offer I've had all day," Joshua responded, a wide grin spreading across his face, ass just a-wiggling as he headed to the bathroom, Nash right behind him.

Chapter Seventeen

Standing naked in front of the bathroom mirror, Joshua looked down his body at the cage on his cock. He brushed his fingers along the smooth surface. As much as he hated the damn thing, he could easily admit that it was working. His morning discipline didn't have the pleasure it once had, but he still craved it like he needed his next breath. There was no way he'd ever not want to feel the sting and burn on his ass, thighs, and back. He also had no unrealistic expectations that the cage was a cure-all for what he was battling in his heart, mind, and soul. The urge to cut had diminished, but only slightly.

The thing was, he was scared shitless to look too deep at his past, at himself, which would be a mandatory journey into hell if he agreed to talk to a psychiatrist. And yet….

Joshua blew out a frustrated breath and looked up to meet his own reflected eyes. "You have to do something." The man looking back at him didn't look convinced. There was fear in his eyes, a fear that swirled around in his gut and caused his breath to hitch. However, he had to face it. Knew to the bottom of his soul that he'd eventually have to or it would destroy him, both physically and mentally.

As he continued to stare at the man in the mirror, he barely recognized him. His long hair clean and shiny, the perpetual dark circles under his eyes no longer visible, and he'd put a few healthy pounds on. Sure, the fear in the green eyes was recognizable, familiar. It had been there since… well, he couldn't remember a time when he hadn't felt at least some fear. But there was something else, something new and foreign shining in his eyes—hope.

For the first time in many, many years, he no longer wished to seek out oblivion. He wanted to stay in the here and now. Wanted to experience life. Wanted to set goals and dream. He wanted Nash and he wanted to be the kind of man that Nash could be proud of.

For so long he'd been playing the game. Doing what others told him to for a place to sleep, a meal, for the oblivion that pain caused.

He'd allowed every person in his life to use him, but it was a mutual arrangement. Now, he truly wanted to make Nash happy, wanted to please him and see that smile light up his gorgeous face. Wanted to feel the soft brush of his touch, hear his praises and compliments. And the most terrifying thing was, he wanted Nash's love. Joshua craved being Nash's boy, but he also wanted to be his friend and lover, two things he'd never been to another person.

He pulled on a T-shirt and a pair of jeans. He adjusted the cage so that it was marginally less uncomfortable before carefully zipping and buttoning up. Today was another first. He and Nash were going on a hike through the hills to a secluded spot to enjoy a picnic lunch. He shook his head and grinned at the image of the two of them sitting on a blanket, little wicker basket filled with finger foods and red-and-white checkered napkins. It was all so very romantic, absurd, and silly, and... absolutely the most amazing way he could imagine spending the day with Nash.

Joshua went to the kitchen and opened the fridge, pulling out the cheese, cold cuts, and pasta salad he'd prepared earlier. He didn't have a cute wicker basket, but the canvas cooler was a more practical option. He put the items from the fridge in the bag and added a bottle of wine, crackers, fresh bread, and condiments, as well as silverware, cups, and paper plates before zipping it up. He whistled the entire time he prepared their lunch, feeling lighter, happier, and more carefree than he could remember ever experiencing. *It's just a picnic, for fuck's sake.* Yeah, whatever, it still made him smile.

"Hey there," Nash said as he stepped up behind Joshua and placed the softest of kisses to the side of Joshua's neck. The press of lips and Nash's warm breath caused Joshua to shiver.

"Hey there," he echoed. "You about ready for our big adventure, Sir?" The title was so natural that, as much as he also wanted to be Nash's friend and lover, the way in which he addressed him would never change. It was too ingrained not to use it. Hell, he didn't want to not use it. It felt right and, to be quite honest, sexy as hell referring to Nash in that way.

Nash wrapped his arms around Joshua's waist, pressing his chest to Joshua's back and resting his head on Joshua's shoulder. "I don't know if I'd consider it a big adventure unless we run into, say, a cougar, a bear, or snakes. But yeah, I'm ready. You?"

"Almost. I just need to get my boots on."

"You think they will be okay? We'll be walking about ten miles round-trip. Maybe you should bring your tennis shoes just in case."

The tennis shoes were just as new and he hadn't had a chance to break in either pair, but the boots were far more comfortable. "I think the boots will be fine, Sir. You did a great job picking them out."

"We can stop and rest as much as you need to. I don't want you getting blisters."

Nash's worry and care caused warmth to spread through Joshua and he couldn't help but smile. "That's sweet, Sir." He turned in Nash's arms, another of his natural submissive tendencies jumping to the forefront when he tilted his chin, begging a kiss, but keeping his eyes respectfully lowered.

Nash didn't deny him. He pressed his lips to Joshua's, tongue teasing at Joshua's bottom lip until he opened his mouth. Joshua moaned with the first slide of tongue, Nash's minty flavor filling his mouth, and he opened wider, wanting more of the addictive kiss.

Joshua was enjoying the warmth of Nash's body against his, the feel of Nash's strong arms circling him, when pain bloomed in his groin as his cock began to swell. He ended the kiss, a little breathless. "No more kisses like that, Sir. My poor dick can't handle it."

Nash didn't release him. "We should probably take it off. We'll be doing a lot of walking and I don't want it to cause you unnecessary discomfort."

Joshua shocked himself when he shook his head, declining the offer before he could think about it. "I kind of like the reminder. It's like you're holding my dick all the time."

Nash gave him a sly grin and reached out to cup Joshua's cock. "I like holding it."

Joshua pushed Nash's hand away. "No touching, Sir, or I won't be able to walk to the car, let alone up a mountain."

Nash gave him a mock pout but conceded and released his hold on Joshua's dick. "Okay, but if it begins to chafe, let me know and I'll take it off."

"Yes, Sir. Thank you."

The car loaded, Joshua slid into the passenger seat and buckled his seat belt. "It's a gorgeous day for a hike," he commented, taking in the scenery around him.

"Not as gorgeous as my hiking companion, but yes, it's nice."

Again, Nash's compliment caused warmth to spread through Joshua. He liked it when Nash complimented him but he still wasn't used to it, nor did he know how to respond to it so he stayed silent, his heated cheeks answering for him.

Nash laughed and patted Joshua's thigh. He fired up the car and pulled out onto the road. It was a short fifteen-minute ride to the hiking trail, but it seemed much shorter as Joshua greedily took in the views around him. He'd been born and raised in the mountains, but he'd taken them for granted. He'd been too busy surviving to stop and enjoy just how beautiful they were.

Once they were parked, Joshua stepped out of the car and went to the trunk to retrieve the cooler. "I can carry that," Nash offered.

"That's okay, I got it, Sir." Joshua slung the strap over his shoulder and adjusted it to sit against the back of his hip.

"Just let me know if it gets too heavy." Nash stepped up to Joshua on the opposite side of the cooler and took Joshua's hand in his, entwining their fingers. "Ready?"

"Yes, Sir." Joshua pulled his shades down over his eyes, shielding them from the bright sunlight. They also hid his eyes behind mirrored lenses, affording him the ability to ogle Nash all he wanted.

Neither said much as they made their way along the winding path. They weren't able to hold hands for most of the trek as the path became too narrow and Joshua found he needed both his hands to steady himself on some of the low-lying trees when the path became rocky and unsteady.

By the time they found a secluded spot that was fairly level to set up their picnic, Joshua's feet weren't hurting, neither was his dick, but he was covered in sweat and breathing a little fast. "Wow, I'm really out of shape," he complained as he dropped the cooler to the ground.

Nash ran his hands through damp hair. He was sweating almost as much as Joshua. "I don't think it's being out of shape so much as that was one hell of a steep hike." He bent over and rubbed his calves. "My legs are killing me. How are your feet?"

"Hot and sweaty, but otherwise unscathed," Joshua assured him. He went to his knees next to the pack and unzipped it. He pulled out two bottles of water, handing one to Nash before he opened his own and took a big gulp. The cool liquid was amazing against his dry throat, and he moaned and took another big drink.

From the small compartment on the bottom of the cooler, he pulled out the sheet he'd stored there and spread it out on the ground. He turned to sit on his butt, untied his boots, and pulled them and his socks off. He moaned again as he wiggled his toes. He stuffed his socks into his boots and set them aside before turning around to see Nash hadn't only removed his boots but his T-shirt as well. Joshua licked his lips as he watched Nash. His head was tipped back, eyes closed as he ran his T-shirt around his neck and down his glistening chest.

"You keep doing that, Sir, and this cage is going to get a whole lot tighter."

Nash opened his eyes and tilted his head toward Joshua. "Wiping sweat gets you hot?"

"Only when you do it. I'd help you out and lap it up, but…." He pointed to his groin so Nash would get the obvious meaning behind it.

Nash went to his knees on the sheet and inched closer to lean over and press his lips to Joshua's. "After we eat, may I suggest we remove it and spend a little quality time in that stream over there?"

Joshua kissed him back. "Best offer I've had all day, Sir." He sat cross-legged and pulled out their lunch, spreading it out between them.

The conversation was light while they ate, talking mainly about the hike, the beauty around them, and the wildlife. Luckily there were only birds, squirrels, and one curious little mouse rather than bears, cougars, or snakes. It was easy, comfortable, and everything Joshua hoped it would be. In fact, it was even more romantic than he'd imagined.

They heard other hikers chatting in the distance, and seeing as neither of them wanted to get arrested for indecent exposure in a state wildlife park, they settled on cooling off in the stream by dipping their toes in it and washing up after lunch. This was fine with Joshua, because now he was leaning back against a fallen log, sipping wine, sitting shoulder to shoulder with Nash. Wine wasn't his favorite choice of drink, but he could easily admit the taste was starting to grow on him.

"It must have been cool growing up in country this beautiful," Nash commented, his gaze toward the mountain range before them.

Joshua shrugged. "I don't know if I'd call it cool. I never really took the time to appreciate the beauty."

"Yeah, I can understand that. A lot of people take things for granted until they lose them."

"Like eating," Joshua muttered. He'd meant to keep that bit of information to himself, but apparently he'd said it louder than he'd thought because Nash took his hand and squeezed it.

"You want to talk about it?" Nash offered.

"Not really, but I would like to hear about your family. What was it like growing up in Michigan?"

"Flat," Nash chuckled. "But, seriously. I had a great childhood. It ended far too soon, but while my dad was alive, I was living the all-American dream."

"I'm sorry. I didn't realize you'd lost your dad."

"When I was twelve. I lost Mom when I was twenty."

"I'm sorry," Joshua said again. He never knew his parents, but he could imagine how hard it would be to have them and then to lose them. That seemed almost worse than never knowing.

"Don't be. I was blessed to have them as long as I did. The doctors had told my mom she'd never have children, but apparently something happened when she hit menopause and surprise, here I am. Mom was forty-seven when she had me and poor dad was fifty-nine. He had to put his retirement plans on hold but he never complained. Spoiled me rotten, he did."

"They sound great."

Nash nodded. "They were. What about your mom and dad?"

Joshua shrugged again. "Never knew them. From what the social workers told me, my mom—I use the term loosely—didn't know who my father was and she was too busy searching for her next fix to be bothered with me."

Nash's grip on Joshua's hand tightened. "What the hell is wrong with people?" Nash shook his head. "I tell you, people should be screened before being allowed to procreate."

"I'm no expert on male-female reproduction, but I don't think it works like that," Joshua snickered.

"Yes, well, it should," Nash said curtly.

"I don't know if it would do any good. The few foster moms I had supposedly went through a screening process and they weren't all that much better than the woman who birthed me," Joshua said, his voice tight, suddenly bitter remembering the places he'd been dumped in.

"I don't even know what to say."

Joshua took a sip of his wine. "Nothing to say. It is what it is. I survived it."

Nash brushed the pad of his thumb back and forth over the back of Joshua's hand. Joshua could tell he wanted to say something more by the way he was staring at him with concern filling his eyes, but he remained silent. Joshua didn't want to talk about it, didn't want the horrors of his childhood to put a damper on the wonderful day they were having together. However, now that the lid had been taken off the box of memories, Joshua knew he wouldn't be able to easily stuff them back in and slide the box away. He turned his head and met Nash's gaze. "What do you want to know?"

Chapter Eighteen

NASH ABSENTLY rubbed at the ache in his chest as he continued to stare at Joshua. So many things he wanted to understand, but as hard as he tried, he couldn't come up with a single damn question to ask. Now that he knew about Joshua's childhood, so many things made sense. The cutting, the abuse he'd allowed from his previous master, his insecurities, his reckless behavior, it all was surely a direct result of his upbringing—or lack thereof.

Nash squeezed Joshua's hand. "I want to know everything about you. What you like, what you hate, what you're thinking. Your hopes, dreams, fears, good and bad, I want to know it all."

"You don't want much, do you, Sir?" Joshua mumbled.

"Just you."

Joshua's eyes went wide seconds before he turned away, hiding them from Nash. He started to say something but snapped his mouth shut.

"I know you have a hard time with compliments, but I'm going to keep making them until you believe me. You are an amazing man and I'm lucky I have you."

"Once again I say, weirdo," Joshua responded, his tone light and joking. He downed the rest of his wine and gathered up their things, storing them in the cooler before going to his feet. "We should head back. We don't want to get caught up here at dark."

Nash pushed to his feet and grabbed Joshua's hand before he could walk away. "If wanting you makes me a weirdo, then I'm completely okay with that."

"Thank you, Sir. And thank you for not asking me any questions about my childhood. It's a stroll down memory lane I'd prefer not to take twice."

"Twice?" Nash asked, confused.

"I've decided to take you up on your offer and see that head-shrink friend of yours."

Nash pulled Joshua into a tight embrace. "You have no idea how ridiculously happy you've just made me. Thank you."

Joshua muttered something Nash couldn't quite make out, but it sounded suspiciously like "at least one of us is." Nash had no crazy notion that this would be easy for Joshua. In fact, it was probably going to be one of the hardest things he'd had to do in a very long time. What Joshua didn't understand was, as hard as it was going to be, Nash was going to be right there to hold his hand and catch him when he fell.

Chapter Nineteen

QUIETLY, SO as not to disturb his sleeping lover, Nash pulled a pair of soft sweatpants and a T-shirt from the drawer. He stood at the foot of the bed, watching the steady rise and fall of Joshua's chest for a moment, enjoying the sight as well as the peace and quiet before heading for the shower.

Getting away had been the perfect solution to the bump in the road they'd experienced in their relationship. It set a slow, easy pace, with lots of relaxing. While Nash had wanted to drop the Dom/sub roles while here, some aspects of it were impossible to forgo. Like Joshua continuing to insist on calling him Sir. Whether it was out of his need to establish the difference between them or because it was a comforting phrase didn't matter. But for the most part, here they were equals, and spending their time together day and night on neutral ground without any outside distractions was exactly what they needed. Simply two men getting to know each other on a personal level. Not that they couldn't have done that in the confines of their contracted relationship, but after Joshua's meltdown and the doubts that lingered about the reasons for his submission, this was the best course of action to take. One which Nash was enjoying.

Nash turned the water on and stepped beneath the warm flow. The water pounded down on his back, waking sluggish muscles. The steam swirling around him was infused with citrus and mint as he scrubbed his body. He slid his hand across his chest, his nipples hardening with the slippery touch. His cock twitched with the arousing touch, and he slid his hand down his stomach and ran it up and down his cock, watching as it hardened against his palm.

"I think you missed a spot, Sir," Joshua pointed out, his gaze on Nash's crotch.

"I thought you were sleeping." Nash kept stroking, thrusting a little. He was so fucking wanton. Totally Joshua's fault. Joshua always made him want. Made him hard.

"The bed was cold, Sir," Joshua complained. He stepped into the shower and moved up close to Nash. He reached out, the tip of his finger ghosting over the head of Nash's cock. "You should have woken me. I could have taken care of this for you in a warm bed."

Nash slid his hand back farther, tugging on his balls a little. The touch made him groan. "I just got started, and it's warm in here too. In fact, it's getting hotter by the second."

"Good point, Sir." Joshua chuckled. He tipped his head back, begging a kiss.

Nash obliged him, pushing his tongue deep into that willing mouth, humming a little, creating a tickling vibration.

Joshua pushed Nash's hand away and took Nash's dick into his fist, tugging and stroking for a moment until he slid his arm around Nash and pulled their bodies close. Joshua rubbed against him, soft fingers moving over Nash's back. Their bodies fit together perfectly, cock to cock, chest to chest. Made for each other.

"Told you it would get hotter," Nash murmured against Joshua's lips. Oh, it was so fucking hot, a fire burning in his belly. Joshua was like a lick of flame to dry kindle, igniting Nash in seconds.

Joshua cupped Nash's ass, tugging him in closer still. "Never doubted you for a minute, Sir."

Their movements sped just a little. Not a feverish pace, but a slow, steady building of need that couldn't be ignored. Nash's cock slid along Joshua's hip and over the ridges of his belly. Nash buried his face in the side of Joshua's neck, licking the water droplets, nipped and sucked his earlobe, making Joshua moan. "God, I love it when you make that sound. Feel it all the way down to my balls."

"This sound, Sir?" Joshua groaned again, deeper this time, and Nash's dick twitched.

"Yes." Nash pushed his hand between their bodies, hips still swaying, movement in perfect sync, and wrapped his hand around their pricks. The friction of cockhead on cockhead had Nash swelling further, breathing a little harder.

Grunts and groans filled the small space, the scent of sex and need swirling, enveloping them in their little private cocoon of steam. Nash sped the movements of the hand that he had wrapped around their dicks, Joshua rutting hard against him. Just as the first hot burst of his orgasm shot from him, Nash took Joshua's mouth in a blistering kiss, feeding him sounds of pleasure and swallowing down Joshua's moans when he followed Nash over the edge.

A shudder ripped through Nash with the last drop of seed as he came. They clung to each other for a moment until Nash's rapid pulse eased, as did his panting.

He moved his lips back to the side of Joshua's neck, nuzzling. "Now that's the best way to wake up."

"Better than coffee, Sir?"

When Nash didn't respond, Joshua lightly slapped Nash's buttcheek. The bit of dominance in Joshua, so unexpected, made Nash jerk, then shake his head, laughing. *Pushy little sub.* He pushed the thought away. Here Joshua wasn't his sub, but it was hard not to fall back into that way of thinking. He'd have to be careful and choose his words carefully. Remember to ask rather than demand. Fight instinct. He placed one last kiss on Joshua's skin and then lifted his head to meet Joshua's gaze. "Yes, better than coffee," he assured him.

The pink in Joshua's cheeks was satisfying, as was the sweet smile.

Nash turned off the taps, grabbed a couple of towels from the hooks, and handed one to Joshua before wrapping the other one around his waist. "Now that I had the good stuff, how about we go indulge in my second-favorite morning treat?"

"I already turned on the coffee pot before I joined you, Sir."

"Sexy and smart. Hot damn, I'm one lucky man." Nash followed Joshua out of the bathroom with a smile.

Nash didn't miss the way the color in Joshua's cheeks deepened. A little compliment went a long way in keeping the man happy. Such a simple thing and one Nash planned on keeping up daily.

"What are you in the mood for, Sir?"

He stepped up behind Joshua and placed a kiss on his warm damp shoulder. "You already took care of it."

"I meant for breakfast." Joshua pulled on his jeans and Nash instantly missed his nakedness. Then again, the man's ass looked pretty good in tight denim too.

"Whatever you make, could you do it naked?"

Joshua laughed and shook his head before he pulled his T-shirt over it. "Not if it includes bacon, Sir."

Before Joshua could step out of the room, Nash grabbed him and pulled him close again. "How about I take you out to breakfast?"

"I don't mind cooking, Sir. I don't like you spending money on me."

"I know, but this is my way of thanking you for the wonderful wake-up. Let's go get something decadent, warm, and gooey."

Joshua tilted his head. "You already had that in the shower."

"Yes, and now I have a craving for blueberry pancakes with warm cream cheese smeared all over them." Before Joshua could say another word, Nash covered his mouth with his. They kissed, one flowing into another until Joshua melted against him.

"What were we talking about, Sir?" Joshua asked, sounding a little breathless.

"Food."

"Mmm-hmm. I could eat."

"Good." Nash took another quick kiss and then stepped back. Ignoring his previously chosen attire, he dressed quickly in a pair of jeans and a soft gray T-shirt.

They hadn't seen another person in a couple of days, and Nash found it a bit sad to leave their little hideaway and rejoin the world. As they walked down the sidewalk toward the café, Nash took Joshua's hand in his and instantly felt better.

The small rural town of Monroe didn't have a lot to offer beyond a post office, a bar, a small church, a general store, and a diner, and apparently they didn't have a lot of gay men in this neck of the woods. They got a few strange looks from the locals—more than likely it wasn't only the sight of strangers in their town, but the fact that they were holding hands. Nash gave no fucks what they thought. He wasn't ashamed of who he was, never had been. Hell, with a handsome man like Joshua at his side, he was downright proud as hell.

The sign outside the Starlight Diner informed its visitors that the place had been established in 1966. Stepping through the doors, it was apparent the place had changed little since then. Red vinyl-covered chairs, Formica table tops, and well-worn black-and-white tile flooring dated the place, but the scents of bacon, warm bread, and coffee welcomed them into the present.

They saw a couple of elderly gentlemen, one dressed in denim overalls, his belly making it impossible for him to button the sides, and the other one rail thin, his sun-weathered face looking as if it were made of leather. Complete opposites in appearance and yet they both had wary expressions when they turned to look who had entered. The waitress, a Polly-Holliday-from-*Alice* look-alike, beehive hairdo and all, gave him and Joshua the same type of greeting.

They seated themselves at a booth near the front window. Nash grabbed a couple of menus from the rack and handed one to Joshua. "Damn, it smells good in here. I'm definitely adding bacon to my plate of pancakes."

Joshua scanned the menu, his eyes huge. "I know, right? I didn't realize how hungry I was until I got a whiff of it." Joshua groaned and pointed to something on the menu. "Did you see this, Sir?"

Nash leaned over the table to see what Joshua was pointing at. He looked up and arched a single brow. "Farmer's breakfast?"

"Oh yeah. Three eggs, bacon, ham, hash browns, and pancakes. Mmm-mmm, I like the way these farmers think."

Nash leaned back, a smirk on his face. "I'll be sure to plow you later and help you work it off."

"Boo, Sir! Bad pun alert."

They were still laughing when Mrs. Polly look-alike came over to the table with a pot of coffee. "Good morning. Would you boys like some coffee?"

Nash turned over his mug, biting down on his lip to keep from laughing when he read the waitress's name tag. "Yes, please, Polly."

Joshua covered his. "None for me. Just water, thank you."

"Sure, Suga," she drawled, popping her gum while she filled Nash's mug. "Y'all know what you want to eat?"

They ordered, Nash adding an extra helping of bacon to his. Once Polly moved away, Nash turned his attention back to Joshua. "So what do you feel like doing today?"

Joshua played with his fork, flipping it over and over on the napkin. "I was thinking that maybe we should go back to your house, Sir."

"Are you so eager for our vacation to end?"

"No, but I overheard you on the phone. I didn't mean to eavesdrop, but I heard you say you had work to do."

"I was talking to Malcolm and the work I have to do is on us. He agrees and he thinks it's a great idea."

"It is, I mean was, a great idea, Sir. I was just thinking, it may be time to go back and consider reevaluating our contract." Joshua looked up briefly before lowering his head again. "I mean if you want to, Sir."

"Are you sure?"

"Yes, I—"

"Wait," Nash interrupted and held up a hand to halt him when Joshua met his gaze. "I need to see your eyes while you're answering."

"Don't trust my words?"

Nash reached across the table and took Joshua's hand in his, entwining their fingers. "I do, but I trust your eyes even more."

"That's actually quite frightening."

"Why is that?"

"It means you can read me."

"It may be a little frightening having someone in your life who can read your feelings, but considering you're ready to go back and commit to me as my submissive, I would think it also brings you a bit of peace in trusting I know what you need without you telling me."

Joshua held his gaze for a moment before a determined expression crossed his face and he nodded. "Yeah, it does, Sir. Still scary, but comforting at the same time. More proof I'm a nutcase."

"You are not a nutcase, just a little lost. But you're finding your way, and with my help, I promise you'll come out on top. Not literally, unless it's because you're riding me."

"Deal." Joshua brought his water up to his lips and winked before taking a drink.

"Oh my," Polly drawled, coming up behind Nash. Nash tensed for a moment, waiting for the sermon about his sexuality being a sin or worse, having to cause a scene when he refused to leave until he'd had his breakfast. But he quickly relaxed when he saw the sly smile on Polly's face when she set his pancakes down in front of him and whispered, "Y'all best be saving that kind of acrobatic for home. This town ain't ready for that kind of dinner theater."

Joshua snorted, then grabbed his napkin as water shot out his nose, which set Nash and Polly to laughing. "I'll be sure to heed that warning," Nash told her between snorts.

"Be sure you do," she responded as she finished setting their breakfast on the table and refilled Nash's mug. "Anything else I can get y'all?"

"No, ma'am." Nash met Joshua's gaze. "I got everything I need right here."

Chapter Twenty

BEING SURROUNDED by the familiar scent of leather should have been comforting for Joshua, but in this setting, he was anything but. His stomach was in knots, and sweat bloomed across his brow and ran down his temples. The fancy leather chair in the even fancier office, sitting across from a stranger who was staring at him expectantly, was enough to kick in Joshua's flight-or-fight instinct.

Dr. Hobson obviously recognized Joshua's discomfort with his line of questioning about Joshua's childhood because he leaned back in his chair, his expression gentle. "How about we try another way? I'd like to try something known as the miracle question that was created by Steve de Shazer."

"Miracle question?" Joshua asked, then shrugged. "I guess it's appropriate since I'm going to need one of those."

"And I may just have the one you need." Dr. Hobson smiled and folded his hands on his desk. "Imagine that tonight as you sleep, a miracle occurs in your life. A momentous magical happening that has completely solved your problem and perhaps rippled out to cover and infinitely improve other areas of your life too…. Think for a moment and tell me, how is life going to be different now?"

Joshua blurted out the first thing that popped into his head. "I won't be here since I would never have been born. Problem solved."

"That's the easy way out, Joshua. Do you really wish you'd never been born?"

Joshua nodded. "Sometimes."

"But you were, so for the sake of argument, let's say you were born. Now, your miracle happened, you wake, and all your problems have been swept away, and you are in an altogether happier place. Don't think about today or yesterday—it's tomorrow, you have a clean slate, not a single problem in your life. Close your eyes."

Joshua leaned his head back against his chair and did as Dr. Hobson instructed.

"Imagine that happy life."

Images from Joshua's past flashed behind his closed lids. He took several deep breaths, struggling to clear his mind and push the unwanted images away. *Imagine that happy life.* For several seconds, the blackness lingered, but slowly it began to dissipate, showing blurred images he couldn't make out, landscapes that appeared unfamiliar. As the mental pictures sharpened, Joshua's recognized the property, the house, the workshop, and the man standing next him, holding his hand with a wide smile on his face.

Nash.

Nash was his happiness? It shouldn't have surprised Joshua, considering the feelings the man was stirring in him as of late. Foreign feelings. The kind that caused his heart to race, his skin to tingle, and an unfamiliar warmth spread through him. Not the kind of heat that hardened his cock or burned his flesh, but the kind he felt in his chest, encompassing his heart.

"Are you imagining it?" Dr. Hobson asked.

"Yes." It was only then that Joshua realized he was smiling and the sensations Nash brought out in him were manifesting themselves simply by thinking about the man.

"What will you do now that you are happy?"

"Submit to him. Love him." Joshua's chest tightened painfully, and he jerked his head up and opened his eyes.

Love? He'd never loved anyone, not even himself. His heart was racing so fast, his head swam and he began to shake. He couldn't be in love with Nash. He didn't know how to love. He hung his head and buried his face in his hands. That moment of happiness was almost cruel. Reality slapped him upside his head, reminding him that he did have problems, he had no miracles, and Nash damn sure couldn't ever truly love someone like him, and even if by some crazy miracle he did, Joshua doubted he'd recognize it or be able to return it. He'd fuck it up; that was his truth. His reality.

Joshua's throat constricted, making it difficult to swallow or to take in a full breath. He pushed to his feet. "I...." He forced down the lump in his throat. "I think I made a mistake coming here. I'm sorry I wasted your time."

"Joshua," Dr. Hobson said gently. "You didn't waste my time. Considering what you've told me about your past, I can imagine that it's hard to imagine your life as happy. But I know you can achieve your goals."

Joshua shoved his hands in his pockets and met Dr. Hobson's gaze. "How can you say that? How can you sound so sure?" God, he wanted to believe it, but not only was he having a hard time thinking about what a happy life would be like, but more importantly, he had a sneaking suspicion that he didn't deserve it.

Dr. Hobson moved around his desk to stand next to Joshua. "You're here. Not because someone forced you to be but because you wanted to. That in and of itself is a huge step." He laid a hand on Joshua's shoulder and smiled. "Beyond that, I can tell by the look in your eyes how badly you want this. I know you can do it."

Joshua stared at Dr. Hobson, not knowing how to respond. He was the second man to seem to have confidence in him. As much as he wanted to believe them, though, he couldn't.

"I wish I had time to convince you. But unfortunately, I have a patient waiting for me. Would you be willing to come back and see me again?"

Joshua shrugged, unable to commit, unsure if he wanted to.

"Go home, talk to Nash, and let me know, but I hope you'll at least give me a chance."

"I'll talk to Nash." It was the only thing he could promise at this point. He shook Dr. Hobson's hand. "Thank you for seeing me."

"It was my pleasure. Please give my regards to Nash."

"I will."

Joshua stepped past the chair and headed for the door.

"Joshua?"

"Yes, sir?" he asked, hand on the knob.

"I want you to keep thinking about that happy life, and the next time we meet, we'll discuss ways to achieve it." Dr. Hobson sounded sure of himself even though Joshua hadn't even committed to seeing him again.

Without another word, Joshua waved and stepped out of the office.

WHEN JOSHUA slid into the passenger seat of Nash's car, the expression on his face wasn't what Nash had expected. He had no unrealistic notions that Joshua would walk out of Cedric's office and be smiling, happy, and cured. But he'd hoped to see at least some hope shining in those green eyes. Instead, the only thing Nash saw was sadness. For an instant Nash wished he hadn't insisted that Joshua talk to Cedric, but he knew that dealing with a painful past was the first step, no matter how sad or difficult. It had to be visited, dealt with, and then and only then could Joshua begin to move on from it.

Nash put the car in gear, and instead of asking about Joshua's appointment, he asked, "You hungry? We can stop at the diner."

Joshua ran his hand down his arm, rubbing it before hugging himself. "I think I'd like to go to your place if you don't mind. I'm not really feeling in the mood to be around people right now."

"Understandable."

The ride home was quiet. Joshua leaned his head against the window. Nash was curious what was going through Joshua's mind, but he didn't dare ask. Not right now. He needed Joshua to know he was there if and when he was ready to talk, though. He parked in the drive and cut the engine. Before Joshua could exit the car, Nash leaned over closer to Joshua, hand resting on Joshua's leg. Nash pressed his lips to Joshua's jaw. "You doing okay?"

"I'm not sure," Joshua admitted without looking away from the window.

"I'm here for you. Whatever you need, you only have to ask." He pressed one more kiss to Joshua's jaw before sitting back.

Joshua turned his head and gave Nash a smile that didn't meet his eyes, more a weak upturn of lip really that spoke of Joshua's sadness. "Thank you. That means a lot to me."

"I mean it," Nash assured him.

As soon as they entered the house, Joshua excused himself, explaining that he was tired and needed to lie down. Again Nash was hit with the overwhelming urge to ask, to push Joshua into telling him about his session, but in the end, Joshua walked down the hall and closed his door without another word between them. It was going to drive Nash crazy, the waiting, the wondering, the worry, but this was Joshua's journey to take. Nash could only stand by and be there if and when Joshua was ready to come to him. Nash stood near the window looking out but seeing nothing but the expression in those beautiful green eyes. He ran his hands through his hair and then clasped his hands behind his head. He sought calm, but after long moments of listening to the rush of blood in his ears from his rapid pulse, he gave up and went to his office to find some help.

He lowered himself into his desk chair and picked up the phone, dialing a familiar number. It rang several times, and he was just about to hang up when Malcolm's breathless voice came through the line. "Hello?"

"Don't tell me you're running marathons now?"

After a slight pause, Malcolm said, "Excuse me? Why in the world would I want to do such a thing?"

"You're out of breath. I figured you must be running or exercising or…."

"Bingo," Malcolm chuckled. "Lucky for you I was merely testing my arm on a whipping boy. The kind made of padded leather and wood rather than flesh and bones."

"And how is your aim?"

"Dead on, although I do find it less satisfying that my leather boy does not respond to my strikes. Anyway, to what do I owe this pleasure?"

"Joshua had his first appointment with Cedric today."

"Wonderful," Malcolm remarked.

"I don't know if I'd agree and I'm pretty sure Joshua wouldn't either. He came out of his session looking worse than when he went in."

"This doesn't really surprise you, does it?" Malcolm asked.

"No, but I still hate it."

"You care about the boy, of course you hate it. Dealing with the past can be a very difficult thing. Did he say anything about his session?"

Nash shook his head, then realized Malcolm wouldn't be able to see the movement. "No, he was quiet on the ride home. I told him I was there for him if and when he wanted to talk. He's lying down right now, and I'm going nuts with worry," Nash admitted. "I wish I could do something for him."

"You already have. He'll come to you when he is ready. Give him time."

"And what am I supposed to do in the meantime?"

"Be patient."

Nash scrubbed his hand over his face and grunted. "Not helping, Malcolm."

"Perhaps not, but it's the only advice I can give you at the moment. You can't force him to talk to you about this, nor can you speak with Cedric. You have no choice but to wait, be patient, and care for him."

"I do care for him, in fact…." Nash swallowed the swell of emotions that lumped into his throat. "I love him."

"I know."

Nash sat back and stared at the phone in shock, then returned it to his ear. "You can't know that. I've only just begun to admit it to myself."

"Call me crazy or a fool but I do believe in love at first sight. You, my friend, have been in love with him since the moment you first laid eyes on Joshua. It's why I knew you were the perfect choice for him, and also the reason I know that, in time, he will heal and return that love."

"I hope so," Nash responded, but the words sounded weak even to his own ears. Nash couldn't stop the nagging feeling that once Joshua dealt with his past, he would want to move on from it and everything associated with it. Including Nash.

Chapter Twenty-One

NASH LAY in bed, staring at the ceiling, feeling more alone that he could ever remember. Joshua hadn't come out of his room. Nash had heard him moving around earlier, but his room had gone silent a good hour before Nash finally gave up and retired to his own cold, empty bed.

He closed his eyes, struggling to clear his head, to push away the dread that had settled into him, but it refused to release him. Each tick of the clock mocked him, another second, then moment, then hour, in which doubt spread through him. The thoughts of Joshua leaving him followed him into an uneasy sleep.

Nash woke from his fitful sleep, surprised to find Joshua kneeling at his bedside, head bowed. A stainless steel mug sat on the bedside table. The unease he'd brought out of the dream clung to him. But Joshua was here, hadn't run from him, and he was relieved. He reached over and ran his fingers over the top of Joshua's head as he smiled. "Good morning."

"Good morning, Sir."

Although he was ridiculously happy and it had only been a bad dream, the chill it produced still lingered. Nash raised the covers. "I'm cold and could use a warm body right about now."

Joshua slid beneath the covers and Nash instantly shifted down, wrapped Joshua in a hug, and rested his head on Joshua's chest. The strong beat of Joshua's heart was like a balm to his soul. He ran his hand down Joshua's back, touching every inch of skin he could reach until he could finally take a full breath and his rapid pulse slowed.

"Are you okay, Sir? You're shaking."

"I am now," Nash admitted and held Joshua a little tighter. "I was worried you were going to leave."

Joshua shoved at Nash and slid down till they were lying on the pillow facing each other. "What made you think that?"

"After you came home and didn't come out of your room, I let my mind wander from one bad scenario to another. Sometimes my mind is my own worst enemy," Nash admitted.

"I'm sorry I made you worry. I had a lot to think about after my session with Dr. Hobson. It's funny, you were worrying about me running, and I've been worrying about you getting tired of my kind of crazy and throwing me to the curb."

"I won't do that, Joshua," Nash promised. "I know you are having a hard time believing it, but I'm one hundred percent committed to us, in whatever capacity you want me. Friend, lover, master, whatever you need. I want to be that person."

"I have no idea how to be a friend or a lover, but I do know I can submit to you." Joshua averted his eyes, his voice low when he added, "At least I can try to."

"That's all I can ask."

Joshua worried his bottom lip, still not looking at Nash.

"I've never been a friend or lover to anyone, only a possession. I honestly don't think anyone has ever really cared about me."

"I—"

"Please, let me finish," Joshua interrupted, meeting Nash's gaze.

Nash wanted to wrap Joshua in a tight embrace, tell him, show him how much he cared. Had there only been sadness in Joshua's eyes, Nash very well might have. But there was a spark of something in Joshua's eyes. Determination? Resolve? Nash wasn't sure, but it was enough to keep him from doing anything except concede. He nodded. "Go ahead."

"I didn't say no one cared to get your pity. It's the last thing I want. It's just...." Joshua blew out a heavy breath and sat up, resting his back against the headboard.

Nash followed his lead and sat next to him, their shoulders touching, and he pulled the covers up over their laps. Nash didn't push, just picked up his coffee mug and wrapped his hands around it, sipping on the much-needed caffeine and waiting—patiently—for Joshua to continue.

"I read our contract last night. I had only skimmed over the wording when you first gave it to me. This time, I actually read it word for word. It's exactly what I need at this moment in my life. I don't need your pity. I need your guidance, your rules. I need a chance to focus on something other than my fucked-up issues. So, I'd like to ask you if we can reinstate the contract with one addition."

"Anything," Nash responded without hesitation.

"I need a couple of hours of free time each week."

"Absolutely. I can add it to the contract. Shall we set specific times each day or perhaps have a code word when you need to step out of your duties as my submissive? I suppose you could safeword or simply tell me you need time." Nash's skin tingled with excitement. Joshua was willing to commit to being Nash's submissive and oh holy fuck how happy that made him. It meant not only was he putting his trust in Nash, but it also meant that he wasn't going to leave. "I think we rushed into things and neither of us was quite ready for that level of commitment. But I am now and willing to commit to it for the full six months. I mean, I'd like it to last much longer and I'll do my best to make sure you're happy and want to continue past the contracted time."

Joshua bumped his shoulder against Nash's and laughed. "Take a breath, Sir."

Nash cocked his head, saw the glint of amusement in Joshua's eyes, and laughed with him. "I was rambling, wasn't I?"

"Yes, Sir, you were. But I got the gist of it. Part of the reason I took so long before I came to you is that I had to get it all set in my head. I struggled back and forth with my decision. I may or may not have slept yet," Joshua laughed weakly. "But whether I slept or not didn't matter. Everything kept coming back to what I needed to succeed in my goals. The answer was you. You're my best chance. I'm willing to see the contract through to the end."

Considering what he'd just heard from Joshua, Nash knew he should be keeping his emotions under control. Joshua was offering the gift of his submission, and unlike the first time they'd discussed the contract, this time Nash heard the conviction in Joshua's voice. However, as hard as Nash tried to keep his expression neutral—he was a Dominant, for fuck's sake—he couldn't hold the smile back that spread across his face. Screw control. He'd reestablish his place of power over Joshua during his discipline session, but first....

In one deft move, Nash had Joshua flat on his back and was laid out on top of him, chest to chest and toe to toe and lip to lip. "I think we should celebrate our new endeavor, don't you?" Nash nipped at Joshua's bottom lip, then eased the bite with the tip of his tongue.

"Have I told you how much I like the way you think?"

"You may have mentioned it once or twice. The question is...." He brushed his lips over Joshua's and then along his stubbled jaw until his mouth was close to Joshua's ear. "Do you like my execution just as much?"

Joshua tilted his head, presenting his neck to Nash at the same time as he thrust his groin up. "Hmm, mind if I get a demonstration before I answer?"

"I should spank your ass for doubting my abilities."

"Don't threaten me with a good time, Sir." Joshua chuckled and thrust up again.

The happiness in Joshua's voice as much as his hard body against Nash's sent a warm rush through him, swelling his heart and his cock, both ready to burst.

It had been far too long since he and Joshua had gotten off, and Nash rutted hard against Joshua as a fevered need overwhelmed him. He took Joshua's mouth in a bruising kiss and moaned his pleasure. Joshua's responding sounds vibrated along Nash's tongue.

Nash wasn't going to last, he couldn't. Without breaking the kiss, Nash slid his hand between their bodies, needing skin. He shoved Joshua's sweatpants down, exposing his long, slender cock. They both hissed into the kiss as their hard shafts came in contact.

"You feel so fucking good," Nash moaned against Joshua's lips.

Joshua's hands landed on Nash's ass, thrusting up at the same time.

Nash's pulse was racing, his breath coming in pants. He planted his hands on the bed near Joshua's armpits and rose up, arching a little to keep full friction on Joshua's cock, the new position allowing him to look at Joshua's face. His green eyes were darkening with lust, white teeth pressing into his kiss-swollen bottom lip. *Fuck!* The man was beyond sexy when he was giving in to his pleasure. The slide of Joshua's cock along his and the scents of sex and sweat and man were a powerful one-two punch to Nash's growing arousal. His orgasm hit him from out of nowhere, stealing his breath and causing his heart to skip a beat as he shot his load over Joshua's stomach and chest, a small amount landing on Joshua's chin.

Nash kept rolling his hips, kept moving, coaxing Joshua to follow. Nash bent down and licked the drop from Joshua's chin. "Come for me." He pushed his tongue past Joshua's panting lips, giving him a taste of what he'd pulled from Nash's body. Joshua sucked greedily, his back arching a split second before he came, feeding Nash his pleasure-filled sounds. Nash swallowed them down as greedily as Joshua had taken Nash's seed.

Nash was reluctant to end the kiss, but his need for air outweighed his pleasure. He rested his forehead against Joshua's, breathing him in until his heart rate slowed and he could take a full breath. He rolled to his side, taking Joshua with him until they were once again facing each other with their heads resting on the pillow.

"I'd say that was one hell of a celebration."

Joshua licked his lips and smiled. "I agree, Sir. A hot, messy celebration."

Nash returned the smile, then ran a finger through the come on Joshua's chest. He brought it to his mouth and sucked it in. "Delicious one too." He kissed Joshua one last time, then patted his ass. "All right, boy. I've coddled you long enough. Time to get this mess cleaned up and then we'll take care of your paddling before you feed me breakfast."

"Sounds like a wonderful plan, Sir."

"Toss me a towel on your way to the playroom, please."

"The playroom, Sir?"

"Yes, I'm much too warm and melty to get up so you'll need to retrieve your favorite paddle for me."

Joshua's smile was brilliant as he slipped from the bed. He stopped by the bathroom long enough to clean himself up and then brought a warm, damp cloth for Nash and dropped it onto his chest. "Don't start without me, Sir."

Nash laughed as Joshua raced out the door, his sweet ass wiggling. Soon it would be a sweet red ass.

Nash cleaned up and tossed the rag to the floor, still smiling as he heard Joshua clomping down the stairs and rushing back into the room in record time. He went to his knees next to the bed and presented Nash with not only the leather and silver-studded paddle Nash had instructed him to retrieve, but also the cock cage.

Nash took the cage and arched a brow.

"I hope you don't think I'm being too forward, Sir. But I was hoping you'd consider putting it on me."

"I thought you hated this thing?"

Joshua nodded his head vigorously. "I do. I hate it with a passion, but…." He lifted his gaze and met Nash's. "You were right, Sir, it did help. And as much as I hate it, you know what I need, and I will try not to question you again."

Nash's chest tightened. He took the paddle and laid it next to himself, then placed his palm against Joshua's cheek and ran his thumb over Joshua's full bottom lip. "It is my job to earn your trust so you won't have to try. But in order for me to do that, I need complete honesty in your words and in your physical responses. Is that understood?"

"Yes, Sir." Joshua sounded sincere.

"Wonderful." He patted Joshua's cheek gently, then patted his own lap. "Present that fine ass, boy."

"Yes, Sir."

Chapter Twenty-Two

JOSHUA STOOD in the center of his room, his flesh still warm and damp from his recent shower. Tonight, Nash would be taking him to the club, the first time he'd been since the night Nash brought him home. It had only been a couple of days since they'd recommitted to their contract, and Joshua was still trying to get used to his schedule and rules. He'd much rather stay home. He didn't want to fuck up and embarrass Nash. But Nash wanted to go and Joshua wouldn't deny him. He was both nervous and excited. It meant a lot to him that Nash wanted to show him off, and yeah, there was a part of him that wanted to throw it in the face of every person who turned up their nose at him, gave him a look of pity or—especially—nasty sneers, like he got from folks like Troy. He would be kneeling at the feet of the most attractive Dom in the place. *My Dom.* The thought made him smile.

"That's a good look on you," Nash commented as he stepped up close to Joshua.

"Naked?"

"No… well, yes, but I was talking about the smile," Nash clarified. "Care to share what you were thinking about that caused it?"

"You, Sir," Joshua said with absolute conviction. The smile he got in return curled Joshua's toes. It looked damn fine on Nash's face too.

"Suck up," Nash sniffed.

"Only stating facts, Sir."

"All right, let's get you dressed before Malcolm scolds me for being late." Nash cocked his head, a mischievous glint in his eyes. "Although, he may forgive me if he learned it was because I had you bent over with my…." He shook his head and pointed a finger at Joshua. "Stop tempting me."

Joshua clamped down on his lips to keep back the snort of laughter that threatened.

Nash walked over to the chair and picked up a pair of leather pants, went to his knees in front of Joshua, and held them out for Joshua to step into. A thrill raced through Joshua at seeing his master on his knees before him and his dick twitched. Nash must have read Joshua's thoughts because he pointed at him again. "Don't get any ideas, boy. Come is a bitch to get out of leather."

"Only if you spill a drop, Sir."

"Cheeky sub."

Unfortunately, Nash didn't try to prove Joshua right. Instead, he slid the pants up Joshua's thighs. Joshua sighed as the soft leather caressed his skin and then moaned wantonly when Nash took Joshua's hard dick in hand and adjusted it within the leather pants, then secured the black laces across it. His ruddy prick looked obscene against the dark ties.

Once Joshua's pants were secured, Nash rolled to his feet and retrieved the black net shirt from the chair. After he had helped Joshua into it, Joshua realized that "shirt" was a generous description. While the mesh fabric covered him from shoulder to wrist, the hem barely reached his belly button. He caught a glance of his reflection in the mirror and pushed his chest out a little more, preening. He'd never worn anything like it or the laced pants, but Nash had a good eye. *I look fabulous, darling.* Joshua rolled his eyes at his silliness. This was a serious night, one in which he needed to focus, not joke around.

Wide wristbands and black leather boots with heavy soles completed the look. They fit perfectly, as did the rest of his clothes—they looked and felt good. Nash stepped back, crossed his arms, and ran a critical eye up and down Joshua's body, a frown marring his brow. Suddenly, he snapped his fingers and went to the armoire, threw open the doors, and started rummaging through its contents.

Joshua's eyes went wide when he saw what was in Nash's hand. He couldn't help but jerk when Nash stepped up behind him and slid the collar around his neck, making sure the small O-ring was in the divot of his throat. He hadn't worn a collar in a long time, and he had mixed feelings about having it around his neck. The last time he had one on had been during a dark period of his life and removing it had been the darkest. Nash buckled it into place, the collar tightening briefly. A strange sound escaped Joshua's lips and his pulse instantly kicked up.

"Too tight."

It wasn't tight, in no way restricting his ability to breathe or swallow, but it felt like a huge weight pushing down on him, and with it came unwanted memories.

Nash wrapped his arms around Joshua, resting his chin on Joshua's shoulder. "Hey, you're shaking. You okay?"

Joshua blinked to dispel the images of another place, another time, another collar. He swallowed down his unease and nodded. "I'm okay, Sir."

Nash ran a soothing hand over Joshua's belly, up his chest to the collar. "Don't let this distress you. It's simply for show. We have a lot of work to do together before we can talk about your actual collar."

"I know but...." Joshua's voice cracked. The idea of being collared by anyone, even Nash, wasn't comforting—it was scary as hell. Collars equaled ownership, possession.... The trembling increased and he struggled to take a full breath.

A gentle hand landed on his shoulder, stroking, comforting. "Look at me."

Panic began to spread through Joshua. *Run!* His heart rate kicked up, sweat trickled down his temples.

"Look at me. Focus. Right here," Nash encouraged.

Joshua lifted his eyes and met Nash's concerned filled gaze.

"That's it. Right here. Long deep breaths."

Joshua focused on Nash, on his soothing touch. It took several minutes, but eventually he pushed the unwanted memories away, stood in the here and now. He took a deep, full breath and blew it out slowly, the trembling easing.

"That's it. Would you like me to remove the collar?" Nash offered.

Just for show, Joshua took another deep breath. "No, I'm okay, sir."

"Are you sure? Would you like to stay home and talk about what just happened?"

Joshua shook his head. "No, Sir. I'm looking forward to going." And he was. He concentrated on Nash, the club, his pride in being at Nash's side.

Nash pressed a gentle kiss to Joshua's temple. "All right. Let's go have some fun and enjoy each other. But we will be talking about this later. Understood?"

Joshua nodded. "Yes, Sir."

Nash kissed him one last time before releasing him. He then walked around Joshua and stood a few feet away, facing him. "You, my boy, are pure fucking perfection."

Joshua's chest swelled with pride, his shoulders going back slightly as he adjusted his stance. "Thank you, Sir."

"I'm going to be the most envied Dom in the place tonight, and I can't wait to show you off."

"I hope I don't disappoint you, Sir."

Nash shook his head. "You never could. All right, let's go make the members of the Underground weep with envy."

Joshua followed Nash out of the room. He didn't know whether they would weep, but Joshua damn sure was going to do his best to make sure they envied Nash by being the perfect sub. Nash deserved nothing less.

EVERY EYE was on him and Joshua as they walked through the club. At least, it felt as if they were. Nash noticed a few subs looking at Joshua with what appeared to be jealousy, others looking to Nash with longing. Whether they were jealous, happy, or indifferent made absolutely no difference to Nash. He didn't need anyone to tell him how lucky he was to have such a beautiful boy walking to his heel.

Malcolm was sitting at the bar, but as soon as he saw Nash approach, he stood and gestured for Nash to follow him. Malcolm stopped at the open door to the back dining room. He held out his arm. "I thought we'd dine in private. We have so much to catch up on. We can enjoy the crowds after."

Nash pecked Malcolm's cheek as he passed. "You simply want to gossip without others overhearing."

"Yes, well, that too," Malcolm admitted, sounding completely unapologetic.

Nash took the seat opposite Malcolm and beamed with pride at the nod of approval Malcolm made when Joshua went gracefully to his knees, his back ramrod straight, head held high, and his eyes respectfully low.

Nash ran his fingers through Joshua's hair, silently praising him before he took his napkin and picked up his empty wineglass.

Malcolm smiled and made a "come here" gesture. "Chardonnay, boy," Malcolm informed Conrad as he approached.

"Yes, Sir." Conrad scurried off.

"When are you going to take that boy under your wing? The way he looks at you, the poor thing is in need of your skilled hand."

"He's much too young for me," Malcolm responded with a dismissive wave. "Your boy, on the other hand, seems to be flourishing."

"That he is."

"And you had your doubts. Worse, you doubted me." Malcolm sat back in his chair with a smug grin on his face.

Conrad returned to the table with a bottle of wine, and while he filled the glasses, Nash took a moment to check on his boy. Although he was sitting perfectly and seemed at ease, his erection had waned, more than likely due to nerves. Nash leaned down and whispered in Joshua's ear. "Go with Conrad, get yourself some water, and take a bathroom break. Be hard for me when you return. Maintain it all evening, and when we get home, I'll tie you to the cross and beat you as a reward." He brushed his lips gently over the shell of Joshua's ear. "Then I will fuck you as mine."

Joshua shuddered. "Yes, Sir."

Nash sat back in his chair. "Conrad, could you escort Joshua to the bar and assure no one steals my boy away?"

"It would be my pleasure, Sir."

Nash sipped at his wine until Joshua and Conrad left. "Okay, I can tell by the way you're vibrating that you're dying to ask me something. Go ahead."

"Joshua looks amazing, but how are his sessions with Cedric going?"

Nash shrugged. "He's only had two visits and is very tight-lipped about what he and Cedric talk about. It's driving me nuts, as you can imagine, but I have to respect his privacy in this."

Malcolm nodded. "I'm sure it's very difficult, but you're doing the right thing. He will come to you in time when he is ready."

"I hope so."

"There you go doubting me again." Malcolm sniffed, then softened it with a curious smile. "And his pain issues?"

"The cock cage is still working quite well, but I fear he is beginning to get used to it. He no longer groans or complains—he's quite eager to have it on, in fact."

"Yes, then you must change it up."

"I know." Nash nodded. "Another thing I'm going to have to approach is his collar."

Malcolm's eyes went wide. "You think that's wise?"

Nash pursed his lips. "Give me a little credit, he is nowhere near ready to be collared. I was referring to his reaction to wearing one tonight. He started to panic when I put one on him. I was able to get him to focus on me and we worked through the panic but whatever the reason was behind the reaction, it has left him shaken."

"Did you ask him about it?"

"Of course, but he wasn't ready to discuss it. Trust me, we will be addressing it, and soon."

"The poor boy," Malcolm sighed. "I hope you are able to bring him peace soon."

"Honestly, Malcolm, I don't know if the boy will ever have it. His past is always lurking just below the surface."

"I must disagree. I think if anyone can help the boy find it, it's you. That he's willing to see a professional to deal with the hardships bestowed upon him while growing up speaks volumes for what he is willing to do for you."

"I don't want him to do it for me—"

Malcolm held up his hand. "There is nothing wrong with him going into counseling to please you or doing it for you. You're his strength, his motivation, and in time, he'll do it for himself as well."

Nash stared at the far wall, unblinking, thinking. Malcolm was probably right. In fact, it was highly probable, and what did it matter who Joshua was doing it for as long as he was? That's what mattered most. He gave himself an internal shake and met Malcolm's gaze. "I hadn't thought of it that way."

"It's a good thing you have me to remind you," Malcolm said smugly. "So, what's next on your to-do list?"

"To be everything he needs."

"What about your needs?" Malcolm asked. "In order for your relationship to work, both of your needs need to be met."

"They are. He does." The truth of it settled into Nash, and he smiled broadly. "Joshua may not be whole at the moment, but every day he learns and grows and heals. My need is to complete him, which makes me whole as well."

"Going to be one hell of a rocky road, my friend."

Nash's smile grew even wider. "The road to happiness usually is."

Malcolm held up his glass. "Here's to a successful journey."

Nash clinked his glass against Malcolm's before taking a sip. It wasn't going to be easy, but Nash was committed. Joshua's healing was Nash's definition of success.

Stay tuned for an excerpt from

Override

An Underground Club Tale

By SJD Peterson

Don't judge a book by its cover….

At over six feet, with a body honed in the gym, auto worker Donavan Gregory is used to people assuming he's a dominant top. Unfortunately, they're wrong, and Donavan's desire to explore his submissive side goes unfulfilled.

Smaller and older than Donavan, Dr. Seth Manning might not look like a typical Dominant, but when the two men meet at Pride, Donavan realizes Seth might be his perfect counterpart. The trouble is, Donavan doesn't have as much experience with the BDSM world as he'd like. What could an educated, handsome, and confident man like Seth possibly see in someone like him? Seth must convince him that despite the differences on the surface, when it comes to kinky fun and discovery, they'll fit together just fine.

Available from
www.dreamspinnerpress.com

Chapter One

AS THE sun began to set on the last night of Pride, Donavan Gregory was surprised his head hadn't exploded from sensory overload. He'd spent the day enjoying the sights and sounds, and—oh holy fuck— what sights they had been. Half-naked men running around laughing, touching, loving in an unadulterated freedom only a celebration of this type could afford.

The afternoon was spent wandering the town, joining in on discussions, meeting new people, taking in the flash and flare of the parade. But it was the fetish booths, the leather daddies, and BDSM demonstrations that kept grabbing his attention. He'd often wondered what it would be like to give up complete control, to kneel at another man's feet, to feel the kiss of his leather. He'd spent countless hours wanking to bondage and kinky flicks, hooked up with a couple of guys who got off on spanking his ass while they fucked him, and yet he hadn't gathered up the courage to take it to the next level.

So it was no surprise when the last rays of the sun disappeared below the horizon that Donavan found himself once again on 5th Street. He leaned against a brick wall, trying not to draw attention to himself. It didn't help that his loose jeans and maize-and-blue college T-shirt made him stick out like a sore thumb among the sea of flesh and leather. Still, he did his best to shrink into the background as much as his size would allow.

People looking at him would, no doubt, find it hard to believe his fantasies revolved around submitting. Standing at six foot two and topping the scales at 230 thanks to good genes and his dedication to the gym, he looked like he would be the dominant partner. That he'd be the one wielding the crop, the one to bind a body, to take charge.

In the center of the road, within a roped-off area, two St. Andrew's crosses had been erected upon a stage. A man dressed in nothing but a pair of tight black shorts was bound to one with his chest pressed against it. A smaller blond-haired man, completely devoid of clothing, stood with his back to the other cross. Donavan's pulse kicked up as he watched the naked man's wrists, forearms, and biceps being wrapped with red ropes. The act was simple yet erotic. The way the Dom moved, the way the ropes slid through his fingers, and the look of concentration on his handsome face kept Donavan captivated.

"You like what you see?"

Donavan jerked his head to the right to find a lean dark-haired man staring up at him with hungry eyes.

Unable to look away from his unwavering gaze, Donavan had the uncanny feeling the stranger was not only looking at him but within him. The man stood about five foot nine and couldn't weigh more than 170 pounds, max. An air of authority and confidence shining in those dark eyes was unmistakable.

Shaking off the strange feeling, Donavan turned back to the demonstration. "Umm, yeah, it's interesting."

Donavan's breath hitched when the stranger inched closer. He smelled of clean sweat, musk, and a rich, pleasing cologne. Donavan watched out of the corner of his eye as the smaller man leaned back, propped his booted foot against the wall, and crossed his arms over his chest.

"Have you ever been bound?"

Donavan shook his head.

"You've thought about it," the stranger said, sounding sure.

But that was ridiculous. No way could this guy know what Donavan fantasized about. Instead of answering, he turned it back on the newcomer. "Have you ever let someone tie you up?"

"I do the tying," he said curtly.

Donavan turned his head and studied the man for a few seconds. He had prominent cheekbones, a regal nose, and his full lips were made for long lingering kisses. While he was handsome, there was nothing physically imposing about him, nor did his attire—black slacks and a finely tailored pale blue dress shirt—scream leather daddy.

"You?" Donavan asked incredulously.

"You know what they say about size not mattering?"

"Yeah."

The stranger tilted his head up, a sly grin curling his full upper lip. "In this case, it's quite true." He pushed off the wall and held out his hand. "Seth Manning."

Donavan shook the offered hand. "Nice to meet you. Donavan Gregory." He started to pull his hand back, but Seth tightened his grip.

As he rubbed his thumb back and forth across the back of Donavan's hand, Seth held his gaze. "Would you like to experience what it's like to be bound, Donavan?" His voice was low and seductive, the tone deeper than Donavan would have expected.

"Perhaps someday."

"There is no time like the present, I always say," Seth countered.

"Now?" Donavan found himself asking, rather than voicing the refusal that first popped into his head.

"Why not? It's Pride. This is your chance to let go, have some fun in a nonjudgmental atmosphere. What do you say?"

Donavan was certainly intrigued by the offer. Given the way his skin tingled and the rapid beating of his heart, his body was certainly on board. He cut a quick glance at the demonstration and the crowds of people. Doubt skittered down his spine. He'd never been an exhibitionist.

"C'mon, Donavan, take a chance," Seth encouraged.

Donavan held Seth's gaze. It was so, so tempting. It certainly wouldn't be a hardship to have someone as good-looking as Seth putting his hands on him.

"Just a little rope play. I won't even ask you to strip." Seth winked. "This time."

"Awful sure of yourself, aren't you?"

"Yes," Seth drawled without hesitation.

Donavan had apparently been influenced by the freedom of Pride, or maybe he'd lost his goddamn mind, but he found himself conceding. "All right, but I'm keeping my clothes on." He pointed a warning finger at Seth. "And no trying to bang me once I'm tied up. I don't do public porn."

Donavan's threat didn't seem to faze Seth in the slightest. He blatantly ran his eyes up and down Donavan's body. "Pity, but you have a deal. Give me a second to set it up."

Seth pushed his way through the crowd, dipped under the roped-off area, and walked up to a large bald man standing near the stage.

Donavan blew out a long breath. *Wow! What the hell have I just done? In public? With a stranger?* He most certainly had lost his mind. He'd always been a private man, never comfortable in the spotlight, but obviously the craziness of the day had worn off on him. It had a damn good hold on him too because he wasn't turning and running like hell. Instead he was standing there, nearly giddy with the buzz of arousal zinging through him, his dick rock hard.

Seth gestured him over, a wide self-assured smile on his handsome face.

Donavan hesitated a moment, then pushed off the wall and walked through the crowd to join Seth.

"Are you ready?"

Apparently, since he was standing there, but Donavan's uncertainty lingered. It was evident in his voice when it cracked. "As ready as I'll ever be."

Seth ran his hand down Donavan's breastbone. "You look tense, and you're shaking. Take a deep breath. This won't hurt a bit, I promise."

Donavan focused on Seth's dark eyes as he inhaled deeply and let it out slowly. A calm settled over him as he continued to hold Seth's gaze. A few more deep breaths and the trembling eased.

"Very good," Seth praised. "Keep that focus on me and the feel of the ropes against your skin. You're in for a hell of a treat."

The crowd around them applauded, and Donavan's attention was drawn to the stage. The man dressed in all leather was taking a bow, with the smaller man kneeling next to him, lowered.

"We have something special for you, today," Rope Guy announced. "Master Seth has agreed to show us some of his knots. Give him a hand."

The crowd clapped and cheered.

Donavan arched a brow in question. "Master Seth?"

"That's what they call me. C'mon." Seth took Donavan's hand and led him onto the stage.

"Donavan, this is Master Rick. He taught me everything I know about knots."

"Nice to meet you," Donavan said.

"Same," Rick said with a wide smile, then turned his head toward Seth. "Modest as always. Anything specific you need?"

Seth considered Donavan for a moment, his lip curling ever so slightly. "I might need a step stool, but that may take away from my big, bad Dom image. How about something for Donavan to sit on?"

"Boy, fetch a chair for Master Seth," Rick instructed.

The man kneeling next to Rick jumped to his feet. "Yes, Sir."

"If you could set it in front of the cross, I'd much appreciate it," Seth said.

Once it was in place, Seth led Donavan to it. "Have a seat, please."

Donavan sat with his back pressed against the cross. His skin prickled with the thought of every person in the audience watching him. His cheeks heated, and he instinctively bowed his head.

"You're a natural." Seth ran his fingers through Donavan's hair.

Donavan's throat was dry, barely able to swallow, so he didn't respond, not trusting his voice. It was ridiculous how his body reacted to Seth's praise. This was nothing more than an innocent exhibition, and yet Donavan couldn't help but think it was more. A first step.

Seth slid a red rope through his hands, drawing Donavan's gaze as Seth's long fingers stroked over the nylon lengths. He then took Donavan's hand in his. The first contact sent a rush of heat to Donavan's groin. Seth positioned Donavan's arm up and out from his body, then wrapped the rope around his wrist and secured it to the cross.

Seth worked silently, a look of concentration on his face as he continued to wrap the rope around Donavan's forearm and bicep. By the time Seth had bound Donavan's other arm, Donavan was breathing hard. He was beyond turned on. It was as though Seth had been working his cock rather than the ropes.

"How does that feel? Not too tight?" Seth asked.

Donavan tested the restraints. They were tight, but not overly so. "No."

"Good. How does it feel?" Seth asked again, his voice low and husky, seductive, like he already knew the answer.

"I like it," Donavan admitted.

Seth's gaze dropped to Donavan's crotch, and he licked his lips. "I think you more than like it. If you like having your arms bound, then you're going to love what's coming next."

A thrill raced through Donavan, causing his dick to twitch. *Jesus!* If it got any better, he was going to come in his fucking jeans. His entire body thrummed with want and need.

Seth situated himself between Donavan's thighs and held out his hand. Someone handed him another length of rope, but Donavan couldn't rip his gaze from Seth. While Donavan found Seth handsome, he'd seen better looking. He'd had the pleasure of bedding a few that could be described as drop-dead gorgeous. But none had captivated him as Seth did. Each brush of Seth's fingers ignited him, made him burn.

Seth's thighs rubbed side to side where they pressed against Donavan's legs as Seth worked, fanning the flames. The crowd melted away, Donavan's entire focus centering on the man before him. A connection was being forged. He was sure Seth felt it too. The thick bulge tenting Seth's slacks gave credence to the belief. Donavan only needed to lean a few inches forward, grab those lean hips….

"Feels good, doesn't it, Donavan? You like being bound and at my mercy." Seth wasn't asking but making a statement. He knew.

A deep rumbling moan escaped Donavan before he could swallow it down.

"That's all the answer I need," Seth murmured. He leaned down, his lips a mere hairsbreadth away from Donavan's ear. "Oh, the things I would love to do to you right now. You are so fucking hot like this."

A shudder ripped through Donavan.

Seth chuckled at Donavan's response as he tied intricate knots across Donavan's chest. Donavan wished he hadn't been so hesitant. *Ha! More like a big scared baby.* And for what? Now he was missing out on feeling the bindings, as well as Seth's touch, against his bare skin. He closed his eyes and imagined it, lost himself in his arousal and the gentle sway of Seth's body. Donavan floated on a wave of pleasure, both erotic and calming, as strange as that seemed. He hung there, for how long he didn't know, but it ended all too soon.

The applause of the crowd snapped Donavan back. He opened his eyes to find Seth standing near the edge of the stage, taking a bow.

Disappointment settled in Donavan's gut when Seth returned and started removing the ropes. It was like being taken to the edge of orgasm and then being denied the ultimate high. He wanted to tell

Seth to stop, beg him to take him to the edge and let him fall, but he'd lost his voice.

Once the ropes were removed, Seth held out his hand and helped Donavan to his feet. The crowd applauded again. Why, Donavan didn't understand. The show had stopped before the climax. Why would that make them clap? Donavan swayed, and Seth slid an arm around his waist to steady him.

"From the first moment I laid eyes on you, I knew you'd enjoy it. Thank you for allowing me to use your body as my canvas. It's quite lovely."

"You're welcome, but it should be me thanking you. It was quite the… experience."

Seth flashed him a brilliant smile.

"Ummm… you wouldn't want to get a drink or something, would you?" Donavan asked, suddenly feeling shy.

"Sorry, but I have a previous engagement." Seth released his hold on Donavan and took a step back. He pulled a card from his pocket. "Call me sometime if you'd like to take it a step further."

Donavan took the card and studied it. *Dr. Seth Manning MD, OBGYN.* "You're a doctor?"

"Does that surprise you?"

"Yeah, it does," Donavan admitted.

Seth glanced down at his watch. "Sorry, I've got to go." He slid his hand around Donavan's neck, pulled his head down, and planted a soft kiss on his lips. "Don't keep me waiting too long."

With that, Seth turned and strode from the stage, shaking hands with people as he went. Donavan stood there dumbstruck as he watched him go. A doctor? A doctor leather daddy? His day was full of surprises. He pocketed the card and, still in a daze, headed back into the crowd.

SJD PETERSON, better known as Jo, is a best-selling and award-winning author of gay romance. She lives in Michigan with her Itty Bitty Kitty and Little Man. She does her best writing when under pressure of deadlines and at 3:00 a.m. when the world is quiet. Jo loves to tell stories about real people with real flaws. The happily-ever-after isn't guaranteed unless it's earned through hard work and growth. Oh, but when it comes, the rewards are all the better!

Facebook: www.facebook.com/SJD.Peterson
Blog: sjdpeterson.blogspot.com
Twitter: @SJDPeterson
Goodreads: www.goodreads.com/author/show/4563849.S_J_D_
Peterson
E-mail: sjdpeterson@gmail.com

CAN DESTINY
AWAKEN A COLD,
DEAD HEART?

IUNCTIÓ CÓPULA
INNOCENCE
TO THE
MAX
SJD PETERSON

On his sixteenth birthday, Francisco "Cisco" Aguilar first sets eyes on Maximilian De Ferrari, owner of Wicked Grounds, an exclusive BDSM club. Cisco has been lost, unsure of what is missing in his life. Over a century old, Max leads a vampire clan, and Cisco is drawn to him in a way he can't explain. The moment he sees Max he knows his quest isn't about what he's been missing, but who.

Five years' wait seems more than Cisco can bear, but he perseveres and on his twenty-first birthday he walks into Wicked Ground. He's unafraid to meet the vampire he's sure is his destiny. Max has been waiting for him, too.

What Max has known all these years, and what Cisco soon discovers, is that more than fate is drawing them together. Iunctio Copula is a powerful binding link capable of restoring cold, dead hearts. With Max and Cisco bound, Cisco will be Max's greatest weakness. Unable to let Max go, Cisco is thrust into a dark world, where he's nearly powerless, left to fight for his life and his future with Max. Worse, he's at the mercy of those who will use him—and hurt him—just to get to the powerful vampire.

www.dreamspinnerpress.com

MY
HOMETOWN

SJD Peterson

Jimmy Brink and Eric Halter grew up together in a small country town. While Eric has always been content with life as a rancher, Jimmy wanted more and moved to Chicago early on to pursue a medical career.

Life has a way of coming back around. When Jimmy's parents decide to retire in Florida, Jimmy returns to his hometown to finish his residency at a local hospital. Flamboyant boyfriend Oliver in tow, Jimmy bumps into his old friend. Eric quickly takes a disliking to Oliver, though, and for good reason. Oliver proves he's not only self-centered but also a cheater.

To complicate matters, Eric finds it more and more difficult to hide his attraction to his best friend. When the opportunity arises, he needs to decide whether to risk their friendship to pursue his feelings… but maybe Jimmy will see there's more for him now than ever before in his hometown.

www.dreamspinnerpress.com

PUP

A GUARDS OF FOLSOM NOVEL

SJD PETERSON

Guards of Folsom: Book One

Micah "Pup" Slayde knows he wants Tackett Austin the moment he lays eyes on him in the Guards of Folsom. Micah wants to have purpose, to be taken care of, and to take care of his Dom—wants to trust him completely, live for him, belong to him. To become his everything. Micah is sure Tackett is the one. The problem is, in order to be the perfect sub, he needs to stay focused, and that's not easy for Micah, who suffers from what he refers to as a "broken brain." Focus and adult attention deficit disorder rarely coexist.

Ever since Ty Callahan and Blake Henderson's collaring ceremony, Tackett's been thinking too much about his own loneliness. Even though Ty introduces Micah and urges Tackett to give him a try, Tackett isn't so easily convinced. He's spent his life pursuing a successful business career, and the subs he dominates almost never enjoy the kiss of his leather twice. Twenty years Micah's senior, Tackett has no interest in taking on and taming such a young and naughty sub—but it's difficult to resist such an adorable pup when he begs.

www.dreamspinnerpress.com

Rival Within

SJD PETERSON

Officer Thomas Webber made a vow of marriage to his wife, a vow to his God to resist temptation, and a vow to uphold the law. But when Tom is forced to shelter a dark-haired stranger from the tornado raging over the county, long suppressed desires are brought to the surface and he is powerless to resist.

Ben Parker has hidden his true nature his whole life. The laws in 1952 are very clear, and to expose himself would mean rotting in jail, shunned or worse, a possible death sentence. Unable to find a job, he turned to crime. Seven years later, he's still angry and tired of hiding who he really is from the world. After meeting Thomas, Ben can envision himself settling down for the first time. The only problem is, he's already forced Thomas to break the law and become his alibi. And then there's the little obstacle of Tom's wife, family, and commitment to the town of Ramer.

Ben knows what he wants, but in order to get it, Tom will have to turn his back on society and the vows he's made if they are to find the happiness they deserve.

www.dreamspinnerpress.com

www.ingramcontent.com/pod-product-compliance
Lightning Source LLC
Chambersburg PA
CBHW060100260626
47160CB00005B/1731